U0063797

校園諺語
全年通！

English Idioms -
All Year Pass!

　　認識 Amy 十二年了，日前應邀上 Amy 家晚飯敘舊，席間她提起正在籌備出版一本新書，並邀請我為她的新書寫序。哇！真是受寵若驚。幾十年來我都以音樂人自居，從沒想過自己的文字會被印刷出版。

　　得知 Amy 的新書是有關英文諺語時，我跟當時座上各位分享了一個有趣的經歷：當年我剛到美國上學時，因為希望能夠更明白當地人的語言，所以選英文課時特意選了有關英文諺語的課，包括 Amy 書中的部分諺語。回港後，畢竟不是全英語環境，因此很多諺語慢慢地忘掉了。

　　2000 年，因為小兒升讀小學，我希望多花時間在小兒的學習上，所以與香港小交響樂團管理層商量，從當年的四月開始就不再擔任大提琴首席。三月為香港芭蕾舞團的《茶花女》舞劇伴奏，是我以大提琴首席身分演奏的最後一次演出。表演結束前有五頁長的音樂選自著名法國作曲家聖桑（Saint-Saens）的小提琴與大提琴二重奏 *La Muse et le Poete*。我特別希望能以最好的演出畫上句號，因此非常緊張。臨近樂曲結束時，我感覺我的小腿和雙腳像是埋在雪地一樣冰冷，直至我拉完最後一個音符，雙腳才一下子回暖。當時令我想起 "cold feet" 這個諺語，意思是一時膽怯，原來人在緊張時，真的會雙腳冰冷。

　　我一直都非常認同 Amy 的英文教學方法，也深信這本與眾不同的書能令讀者對學習英語更感興趣。

劉儀 Yvonne Yee Lau Kam
香港小交響樂團前首席大提琴

　　對喜愛的事物懷抱熱忱而歷久不衰，並非易事，只有少數人能夠通過時間的考驗，成功實現夢想。

　　從認識 Amy 的第一天起，已感覺她有一份濃濃的赤子心，滿腦子都是夢想，眼眸裏還不時帶着憧憬的神色，熱切期待著實現夢想的一天。她對很多事物都有濃厚興趣，語文是其中一項。在大學修讀翻譯系畢業後，她便投身報館、出版社和教育機構等工作，及後又在報章撰寫學習英語的專欄，全部都離不開文字和語言。多年來，她全身投入英語教學，將所學與人分享，培育新一代，把興趣變成終身事業。

　　由於長時間涉足香港的英語教育，加上對專業的堅持和執著，Amy 累積了不少獨到的心得，對學習者的需要和面對的困難瞭如指掌。今天見證了她的著作面世，實現夢想，為她感到萬分高興；也慶幸一本實用而有趣的英語工具書的誕生，造福莘莘學子。

朱溢潮 Buston Chu
香港浸會大學特邀教授
前大昌行集團總經理（市務及企業傳訊）

　　我由入讀演藝學院的第一天開始，便學習到 "The show must go on" 這句說話，意思是無論遇到任何情況，台前幕後所有人員，必須讓演出開始、完成。

　　這是一份專業精神的呈現，但有時候也是舞台工作者的痛苦。試過有演員在音樂劇演出中受傷，之後幾天的演出，要撐着拐杖上台，還要載歌載舞；更有朋友因為有演出在身，錯過見親人最後一面的機會……

　　人生如戲，戲如人生，其實 "The show must go on" 的精神，在生活層面上可以給予我們很大的動力。無論遇到多大的困難，生活仍然要繼續，當我們克服一個又一個的難關後，"The show" 自然會變得精彩。

　　很高興得知 Amy 將會出版有關英文諺語的書籍《校園諺語全年通》，題材充滿趣味，令人期待。常言道「藝術來自生活」，但其實「語言」同樣來自生活。執筆期間，剛剛得知港式英語 "Add oil" 已確定列入牛津詞典！學習一種語言，會隨着生活而演變，是一件很有趣的事情。期望本書會讓更多讀者，體會到不同語言之間的種種微妙關係。

劉浩翔 Elton Lau
iStage 劇團藝術總監

在這個變化萬端的年代，人既要讀萬卷書，也要行萬里路。年青人要多點人生歷練，除了能擴闊眼界和更易抓緊機遇之外，經歷也能令人對自己的人生看得更透徹、生活過得更美好。

學生年代的我只會背誦所有課本，即使知其意義，也未能融會貫通。但這些年來，我走過世界的邊端、攀過上世界最高點，也到過世界盡頭的南極⋯⋯再翻看一些成語、諺語、金句，赫然發現自己陶醉着咀嚼一字一句背後蘊藏的深層意義，就好像釀酒要釀夠年份才能散發醇香。

誠意推薦你閱讀此書，希望你會對文字有另一番體會、多一番喜愛，日後再欣賞一些諺語時，除了能想起自身的經歷外，也能多一番喜愛人生考驗的悸動。

吳俊霆 Elton Ng
物理治療師
香港第二位完攀世界七大洲八頂峰的攀山家
香港十大傑出青年

Foreword 前言

　　很多人説學習英語很困難和沉悶，每天都要埋頭苦幹，只管做練習、對答案、做改正，然後又不斷重複。久而久之，學習過程便容易流於機械化，使我們忽略了整體的應用，甚至大大降低我們的學習興趣。

　　這樣學習英語，當然會在書寫和説話時變得較為生硬，更遑論運用自如。其實只要在學習上多加入日常生活原素，放膽嘗試在不同的處境裏運用英語，便不單能提升吸收能力，更可增加不少學習趣味；諺語可説是當中的好幫手！

　　英文諺語由一組單字組成，通常（但不一定）包括一個動詞或一個類似動詞的結構，與其他字構成固定的組合，用來表達一個特別的意思。由於本質上屬於非嚴肅用語 （informal expression）， 諺語通常用在日常對話中；而在書寫時雖然也用得着，卻緊記「可用」但不要「濫用」，寧缺莫濫。遇見諺語時，或許可以從字面猜想到意思，例如説某人正在 "looking for a needle in a haystack"，就表示該人在尋找極難尋獲的東西。不過，有些諺語卻會令人摸不着頭腦，例如常作為例子的 "kick the bucket"，其實是「死亡」的意思！

　　正如上文所説，在「寫」和「講」英語時要避免顯得生硬，學習時不妨多觀察和利用實際場景，從諺語出發可以説是入門首選。就讓我在這裏講一個親身經歷：

　　我早前外遊，在路上騎單車時不慎跌倒，傷勢不輕。還記得頭部着地一刻，眼前一片漆黑，「回魂」後看見外子被我當時的樣子嚇得目瞪口呆。（When I came to, I could fuzzily see my husband looking very concerned. He was frozen to the spot!）我在想：「今次死定了！」（That's the end of the world ！）。真是 "a close shave"，中文即「險過剃頭」，因為差點兒就可以糟糕十倍！ 一個對我來説並不十分有趣的經歷，卻可以讓我聯想到幾個頗生動有趣的諺語。

　　究竟怎樣才可運用正確、恰宜，就要看你是否理解諺語背後的意思，包括中、英文世界之間的文化差異，例如 "going down the rabbit hole" 的出處是十九世紀作家 Lewis Carroll 的名著 *Alice's Adventures in Wonderland*，意思是進入了一個奇異、混亂、不合常理的環境以至難以自拔。雖然不是每一個諺語背後都有一個明確的出處，但無論如何，多了解其意思和用法，相信運用時會更得心應手。

　　這本書收錄了 52 個常用英語諺語，寓意一年 52 個星期、甚至 365 天都可以用得上，題材多環繞學生一年的活動和生活。即使讀者不是學生身分，也會發現本書的內容全部都是常用的諺語，部分更可以輕易聯想到近似的中文成語，例如 "skating on thin ice" 即「如履薄冰」的意思。

　　希望讀者能享受閱讀這本書，從而多想像多運用，使學習和應用英語成為生活中的一部分。

　　本書內容定有不少可以改進之處，希望各位讀者不吝嗇賜教，以便更正。

Acknowledgment 鳴謝

寫一本小書，想不到能夠邀請到這麼多友好的幫忙。劉儀小姐、朱溢潮先生、劉浩翔先生及吳俊霆先生分別為本書寫了推薦序，讓我感到十分榮幸。

劉儀小姐是大提琴演奏家，造詣非凡，而且桃李滿門。序中她提到留學時學習英諺的需要，以至後來有關 "cold feet" 的親身經歷，生動有趣，令人印象深刻，堪稱真實教材。

朱溢潮先生任職商界高層管理人員多年，卓有成就，現在更於大學兼職教席，栽培後進。我青葱歲月時得到他許多教導指點，如他所說，希望今天我仍懷赤子之心，勇於嘗試新事物。

劉浩翔先生活躍於香港話劇界，對推廣話劇藝術滿有理想和熱忱，更是編、導、演無所不精。他機智幽默，對語言有着敏銳的觸覺，一語 "add oil" 也提醒了我要繼續努力，為理想前進！

吳俊霆先生是一位專業的物理治療師，更加廣為人知的是他在登山運動方面的成就。他於 2017 年成功登上珠穆朗瑪峰之巔，即使登上世界第一峰也從不炫耀，給人的感覺總是一個不怕困難、永不言棄的謙謙君子，是我最敬佩的人之一。

此外，在文稿方面，Mr Patrick Wood 為這書的英語對白部分提供了很多寶貴意見，令我獲益匪淺，感謝至深。劉勇強先生友情客串，審閱了部分中文稿，提出不少有用的建議，在此致以感謝。很感謝 Miss Jessie Choi 細心協助整理一疊一疊凌亂的手稿及對原稿作出潤色，文稿得以迅速成形。

還要多謝另外兩位説得一口漂亮英語的年輕人 Miss Maxine Poon 和 Mr Richard Wong。他們能夠抽出時間到錄音室與我一起錄音，過程樂趣無窮。更有賴萬里機構的編輯、設計、行政人員的支持，使這書順利付印，在此一一感謝。當然，書中仍然有的任何瑕疵與錯誤，全歸咎於我自己。

最後，還要多謝外子、兒女的鼓勵和支持。無言感激，只想將這書獻給他們。

Contents

Contents

Contents

July-August

Summer Holidays

Back to

Chapter 1

September

School

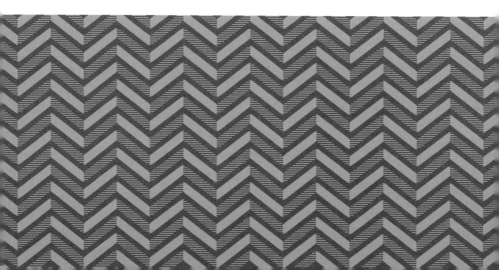

贏在起跑線

Get a head start over somebody

背景 Chloe 當選學生會主席。

Ted

Hi, Chloe! Many congratulations on being elected as the new Chairman of the Student Union.

Chloe

Thanks, Ted! I never believed I could win at the election. The other candidates were so strong.

Ted

Now that you'll officially become the new Chairman next month, have you got plans on picking the members for the new executive committee?

Chloe

Sure! I've already arranged for an informal meeting with like-minded fellow students next week so that I can **get a bit of a head start** before the inauguration. Ted, it sounds like you are ⋯

Ted

Chloe，你好！恭喜你獲選為學生會的新任會長。

Chloe

謝謝你，Ted。我怎會想到真的會當選呢！其他的候選人都是很有實力的。

Ted

下個月你就正式上任了，執委會的成員是否已有頭緒？

Chloe

當然有！我已經安排好下個星期與志同道合的同學碰碰面，好使我能夠在就職典禮之前安排妥當，希望**有個好開始**。Ted，聽來你好像有興趣⋯⋯

意思是比別人提早開始，從而佔優。

用法有點兒像先拔頭籌，例如 A 隊在比賽的首個回合勝出，可以在第二個回合先人一步開始。"Get a head start" 用法不限於比賽或爭逐，這裏的佔優可以是與別人比較，亦可以指自己想儘早作好準備，使以後的工作更為順利。

1) To get a head start over his class, Malcolm has read all the textbooks in the summer holidays.

2) "Make sure you set a fast lap to get a head start in the race," said the team strategist.

3) Mary's worried that others would get a head start over her if she doesn't sign up for tutorial classes.

4) Peter knew well that if he had kept procrastinating, others would have got a head start over him in class.

5) Even if you don't want to have a head start over your classmates, you still need to finish your holiday homework before the new school year begins.

成績彪炳

Pass with flying colours

背景 學期初考試前數星期，
Ted 在圖書館碰到 Chloe。

Ted

Hi, Chloe! I knew I will see you here in the library. You don't miss any time for studying.

Chloe

Oh Ted! Is that a compliment? I finished my lunch quickly and it's such a hot day today, so coming to the library seems the best thing to do. I love the air-conditioning!

Ted

So are you already studying for the exams? They are weeks away!

Chloe

Yes, I am. I prefer studying and revising on a gradual basis and don't want to do it in a hurry. I find this easier in fact!

Ted

Right. Preparedness is the key. No wonder you always **pass exams with flying colours!**

Ted

Chloe，你好！我早知道會在圖書館見到你。你總是每分每秒都在努力讀書。

Chloe

真不知道你是讚我還是在笑我呢！我剛剛吃過午飯就來這裏。外面這麼熱，我覺得來圖書館是最佳選擇了。我多麼享受這裏的冷氣呢！

Ted

你開始準備溫習大考了嗎？還有好幾個星期才開考啊！

Chloe

我開始溫習了。我比較喜歡循序漸進地讀書溫習，最怕匆忙趕課。我覺得逐少溫習會容易些。

Ted

明白了。準備充分是最重要的，怪不得你每次考試都**以優異的成績名列前茅**了。

意思是以優異成績通過考試。這諺語亦可用來形容考試以外的事，如勝出比賽、完成工作、通過測試或檢查之類。除了用 "Pass" 一字，亦可用 "come with" 或 "come through"。

諺語可追溯至十七世紀末。船隻有不同原因出海，但途中都可能遇上風浪，能夠順利回航返抵家鄉是一件值得歡天喜地的事。船員安全泊岸時會升起船上顏色鮮艷的旗幟，表示已經歸來。"Flying colours" 就是代表這個旗幟在飄揚的情景。

1) James knows that he has to pass every exam with flying colours if he wants to study in Oxford.

2) Teachers were let down by Elena's mediocre results as it had looked promising that she would pass with flying colours at the DSE!

3) Time is running out. You must work hard so you can and finish your project with flying colours.

4) Trevor miraculously passed the driving test with flying colours even though his coach didn't have high hopes for him!

5) Our presentation was great. Our department has come through the selection process with flying colours.

1.3

使某人加入隊伍

Bring somebody on board

背景 交專題研習的限期快到，同學仍在惆悵。

Jessie

I'm still figuring out how we can submit the project to Miss Cheung on time. Its deadline is just a few weeks from now, and don't forget that we have to make a model for presentation in class. None of us are any good at that!

Mandy

My brother is very good at making and fixing things. He once made a miniature space station for my birthday.

Jessie

That's good to hear! Do you think you can bring him on board? We'll try our best; but he can help us do the rest!

Jessie

我仍然在惆帳怎樣可以準時交專題研習給 Miss Cheung。距離交功課日期只有幾星期，我們還要做一個模型在班上講解。我們沒有人懂得如何做啊！

Mandy

我哥哥的手作和修理東西很棒，他曾經造過一個小型玩具太空發射台給我做生日禮物。

Jessie

好極了！不如**請他加入幫忙**，我們做好本份，他就彌補我們的不足吧！

意思是希望說服別人認同一些想法，使他加入隊伍幫忙或支持。上船時英文叫 "get on board a ship"，即是如果你肯上這艘船，就意味你已經同意與其他船員一同經歷這個船程。大都是用在正面的工作，例如籌組新政府、團體或隊伍，招募人才加入；而並非「拖別人落水」的意思！

另外，當有新人加入公司時，上司往往會對新下屬說："Welcome on board!"，就是歡迎他加入的意思。

1) Do you really think it's a good idea to bring Jake on board our graduation trip! I doubt he would be good company.

2) Henry has been promoted to the position of General Manager of the company. He wants to bring the best people on board to help him.

3) Hannah has almost finished her job assignments in the new Student Union. Now she needs to bring the right schoolmates on board.

4) This Maths project is so difficult, I think we need to bring Kenneth on board and be our leader!

5) "Thanks for taking me on board! I will try my best in this team," said the new leader.

出手相助
Give somebody a hand

背景 大清早，Jessie 在學校見到 Chloe 拿着一大疊報紙上課室。

Jessie

Good Morning, Chloe! Do you need me to help you carry the newspapers? They look heavy and difficult for you.

Chloe

Thanks, Jessie! Yes, please! They are heavy. Everyone in our class orders newspapers, so this is routine work for me every Monday, Wednesday and Friday morning.

Jessie

I see. I come to school fifteen minutes earlier every Monday and Wednesday, I can **give you a hand** on these two days.

Chloe

Are you serious, Jessie? This is 7:30 in the morning. Can you really make it?!

Jessie

Not a problem. I'm here anyway!

Jessie

早晨，Chloe！要我幫忙拿報紙嗎？看來很重，你也拿得辛苦。

Chloe

謝謝你，Jessie！麻煩你了！真的很重，班裏人人都訂閱報紙，每逢星期一、三、五都一樣，已成了常務。

Jessie

原來如此！其實我每逢星期一和星期三都會早十五分鐘到達學校，這兩天我可以**幫你一把**，一起取報紙的。

Chloe

是真的嗎，Jessie？那就太好了，不過是早上七點半，你是真的可以嗎？

Jessie

沒問題，反正我已經在學校等着早會開始呢！

意思是「給幫忙」，就像給別人多一隻手做事，與 "Do somebody a favour" 相似。但不要混淆另一個諺語 "Give somebody a big hand"，意思不是幫了一個大忙，而是指用力拍掌來表示欣賞。

1) "Can you give me a hand? These books are for display inside the hall!"

2) My mother is always busy with housework. I give her a hand whenever I can at home.

3) Jonathan is a very kind and generous person. He's willing to give his friends a hand when it comes to money matters.

4) Chloe always volunteers to give a hand to the needy at school.

5) Please give a hand to disadvantaged people in our society who are in need.

1.5

脫「殼」而出，參與活動

Come out of your shell

 Natalie 是中二插班生，在迎新派對裏碰到中四級的 Valerie。

Valerie

Hi, I'm Valerie. I'm in 4A. How do you do?

Natalie

I'm Natalie of 2B. I'm fine. Thanks!

Valerie

Why are you sitting alone in this corner? We are about to start with some games in a minute, why don't you join us?

Natalie

Thanks, Valerie! I'm new here and I don't know anyone yet. And this school is so big. I don't really have any idea of where to start.

Valerie

You're right, our school is big and we have lots of regular activities. I'm a student ambassador. Let me show you around. Just **come out of your shell** and you'll love learning in this place!

Valerie

Hi，你好！我是 4A 班的 Valerie。

Natalie

Hi，我叫 Natalie，2A 班新生。你好！

Valerie

為什麼你一個人坐在角落？活動快要開始了，你不如加入我們吧！

Natalie

謝謝你，Valerie！我是新生，學校這麼大，我仍未到過所有地方，或了解有什麼活動可以參加！

Valerie

對呀！我們學校很大，課外活動又多，初來報到的同學是要花點時間了解的。我是學生大使。不如你快快**出來參與活動**，跟我參觀一下學校，你一定會很喜歡這裏的學校生活！

諺語裏的 "shell" 一字，原本用來指動物如烏龜、蝸牛之類的硬殼。動物的硬殼大多用來保護身體免受外來傷害。如果把同一個概念放在人身上，就是指用方法保護自己。"Come out of your shell" 就是指不用害羞，要多走出來認識其他人，參與社交活動，就像一隻烏龜把頭伸出硬殼才可以接觸外面的世界。但是我們用的時候要盡量顧及對方的感受，因為傳統上除了長壽，中國人都不喜歡給人形容與烏龜有關的。

要留意的是，有另一個諺語 "come out of the closet"，意思差不多，都是要開放自己，接觸其他人，但用起來要小心一點，因為通常用來形容有特殊性傾向的人站出來告訴別人自己的傾向，香港直譯成「出櫃」。

1） Johnnie used to be shy, but has come out of his shell since he started working in this coffee shop.

2） This orientation party is for newcomers to encourage them to come out of their shells.

3） The freshmen's week in the university is a good opportunity for students to come out of their shells and meet new friends.

4） "Hey, Jack! You've been here for a month already. Come out of your shell and meet people from other departments."

5） I'm confident that Melanie will come out of her shell at the Christmas party.

School

Chapter 2

Events

破了紀錄

Break the record

 背 景　Malcolm 預備學校水運會的選拔賽。

Sharon

Hi, Malcolm! They are selecting the swimmers for the Swimming Gala next week. Are you confident on being selected?

Malcolm

You know I've always loved running, and swimming is my new challenge. But I've been practising quite a lot these days for the selection. Hope it helps.

Sharon

Don't worry, Malcolm! You've always been sporty and you're strong too. I've seen you swim like a fish. I think you'll even **break our record** next week.

Malcolm

Will I?! But I have to be very careful not to get sick now or else I'll be in big trouble!

Sharon

Malcolm，下星期就是水運會的選拔賽，你有信心嗎？

Malcolm

你知道我一向喜歡跑步，游泳是我的新挑戰。我近來積極練習，備戰選拔賽，希望有幫助啦！

Sharon

別擔心！你好動，又強壯，我見過你游泳，如魚得水，有姿勢又有實際，你真的不用擔心不能入圍，你還可能會**破我們的紀錄**！

Malcolm

會嗎？！但現在要加倍小心不要生病，否則就前功盡廢了！

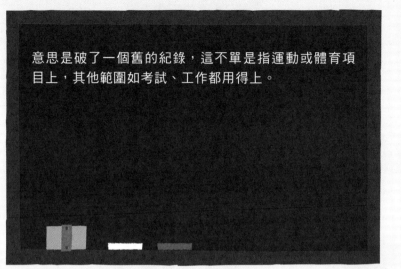

意思是破了一個舊的紀錄，這不單是指運動或體育項目上，其他範圍如考試、工作都用得上。

1) My dad used to be a swimming coach and he has even broken the record of his company's swimming team.

2) Charlotte has had special training in distance running for nine months already. She wants to break the record of her school.

3) Danny started hiking every other day three months ago. He's not only much healthier now, but has also broken the record of the top hiker in his class.

4) With his handsome face Edward has successfully broken the sales record of the boutique by selling dresses to a group of teenage girls.

5) A male student has broken the record in Hong Kong by being the first student who has attained 5** in nine subjects.

歡喜若狂

On cloud nine

背 景 Sharon 被老師挑選為校際辯論隊隊長。

Ted

So you're selected, Sharon! You are now representing us at the Inter-school Debate. Congratulations!

Sharon

Thanks, Ted! It's my honour. But I feel nervous about this. You know I don't have too much experience at inter-school contests. I'm a green horn here!

Ted

Don't worry, Sharon! Our teachers have plenty of experience in this contest. We got very good results in the previous years.

Sharon

But I still lack confidence. Worse still, I'll be the captain of the team.

Ted

Your English is profound and you have such a logical mind. I'm sure with the teachers' help, you'll perform well. Haha! If I were you, I'd be **on cloud nine** now!

Ted

Sharon，都說你會被選拔為學校代表出戰校際比賽啦！恭喜你！

Sharon

謝謝你，Ted！我都覺得好光榮，但又覺得好緊張。我沒有太多辯論比賽的經驗，是新丁！

Ted

你有什麼好擔心呢！你雖然沒有經驗，但我們老師有豐富經驗，學校在這些年來的成績都很好！

Sharon

但我仍然沒有信心，更糟糕的是老師要我做隊長！

Ted

你的英文好，思辨又敏捷，還害怕什麼！換轉是我，我一定會**歡喜若狂，開心透**了！

意思是感到非常高興，歡喜若狂！

美國的天氣部門 "US Weather Bureau" 在 1950 年代把雲分成很多類型和級別，而我們較為熟悉的有 "Cumulus"「堆積雲」和 "Nimbus"「雨雲」。"Cumulonimbus"「積雨雲」可說是兩者的結合。這種雲的高度可達十公里高，是最高的一種雲。而這種雲的外觀亦十分美麗，美國氣象部門稱之為第九級。這個諺語用來形容心情亦頗為貼切，像人們常說的「心情靚」、「好 high」！

1) Chloe has got a teddy bear for birthday from her best friend. She's literally on cloud nine.

2) Now that Jamie has got a job offer from this prestigious company. Her dream has come true and she's on cloud nine!

3) Katie just received her scores for the Grade 8 piano exam today. She's got distinction! No wonder she's on cloud nine!

4) Henry and Linda are looking forward to their honeymoon in Europe next week. They're on cloud nine!

5) Malcolm has finally got the offer from his priority university this morning. It's his first choice. His whole family is on cloud nine!

兩全其美

Having the best of both worlds

 媽咪的公司要搬遷了，究竟是好事還是壞事呢？

Mum

I've got something exciting to tell you! My boss has just confirmed that our office is moving to a new place in the next quarter. It'll take less than twenty minutes to get there from home.

Dad

That's really good news! So you can save a lot of time travelling. You can even pick up our daughter from school after work.

Mum

You're right! I can **have the best of both worlds** then!

Mum

我有一個好消息要告訴你，我的老闆今天正式宣佈，我們的辦公室將會於年底搬遷，新地址十分便捷，到時候上班只需二十分鐘！

Dad

這個真是天大喜訊，到時候你可以大大節省交通時間，還夠時間接女兒放學呢！

Mum

真的是**兩全其美**！

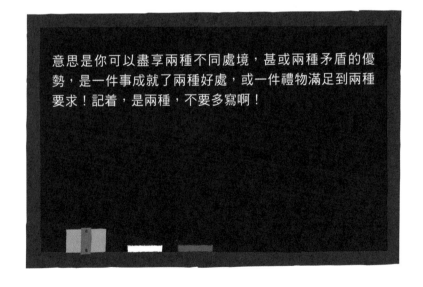

意思是你可以盡享兩種不同處境，甚或兩種矛盾的優勢，是一件事成就了兩種好處，或一件禮物滿足到兩種要求！記着，是兩種，不要多寫啊！

1) I have two young children and I work as a part-time tutor at a learning centre. I can take care of my family while enjoying my working life. I have the best of both worlds.

2) Jennifer wants to go swimming at the beach but she doesn't want to be exposed to the sun. She can't have the best of both worlds!

3) My cousin has a sweet tooth. She loves eating desserts and cold drinks but she keeps complaining about gaining weight. She can't have the best of both worlds!

4) My boss is letting me take my holiday before Christmas this year. My wife and I can now book our tickets more cheaply and we can also enjoy a longer holiday. Hooray! We can have the best of both worlds!

5) This house is located near a park and a library. If we move here we can exercise and read more often and so we have the best of both worlds.

在傷口上灑鹽

Add insult to injury

背景 Mandy 一向喜歡說挖苦人的話，這次在圖書館看見受了傷的 Malcolm，看來又會有事情發生了！

Mandy

How strange to see you here in the library, Malcolm! This weather is perfect for running. But this doesn't matter to you anymore! You've hurt your leg and lost your place in the heats anyway! You'd better stay in the library for the rest of the school year!

Malcolm

Thanks for reminding me about my failure and my injury! So do I need to take your advice seriously? Or are you **adding insult to injury**?

Mandy

Malcolm，今天天氣真好，最適宜跑步。但想不到會在學校圖書館見到你呀！不過天氣怎麼樣也跟你沒關係吧，反正在上一次比賽你不只輸了，更傷了腳，還是圖書館適合你多一點！哈哈！

Malcolm

謝謝你提醒我的失敗。你來是為了安慰我還是只是想**在我的傷口上撒鹽**！

意思是有人做了一些事情或講了一些說話，令到一個原來已經頗不理想的境況更為糟糕。有時候不一定會牽涉另一些人，例如你病倒了，在回家途中突然下起雨來，而你又沒有雨傘，就可以用上這個諺語！

1) Melody is quite weak in Mathematics. To add insult to injury, she got sick on her Maths exam day.

2) Ryan lost his championship at the Inter-school debate competition. To add insult to injury, his schoolmates blamed him for not being a good leader in the team.

3) "It seems that you have tried your best already, but you're still behind me in the test. Try harder next time!"

"Are you adding insult to injury, Chris?"

4) I'm very worried about my job recently. My new boss is very fierce. To add insult to injury, I made a mistake at work yesterday. I think I'll be fired very soon.

5) Sabrina is already late for school. To add insult to injury, she forgot to bring her Student card and locker key!

給他一個教訓

Teach somebody a lesson

 Danny 剛收到測驗成績。

Valerie

Danny, why are you here, alone at the corner of the playground? You look very sad.

Danny

You're right! I'm really sad. Our teacher has just given us back the test papers we did last week. I got very low marks.

Valerie

How come? You're always good at Maths!

Danny

It's all my fault! I did a very stupid thing the night before the test. I kept playing computer games and even drank a cup of expresso to keep myself awake. In the end, I couldn't sleep the whole night and my brains were empty during the test.

Valerie

Oh dear! Computer games plus coffee. That's really too bad!

Danny

This has taught me a big lesson!

Valerie

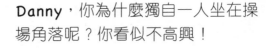

Danny，你為什麼獨自一人坐在操場角落呢？你看似不高興！

Danny

是啊！我真的很不高興！剛剛派了數學測驗卷，我的分數很低。

Valerie

真的嗎！你一向是數學強項，為什麼今次失手呢？

Danny

都是我不好，我在測驗前一晚做了一件很傻的事。我整晚在玩電腦遊戲，為了提神還喝了一杯特濃咖啡，所以整晚都睡不着覺。測驗當天整個人都十分混沌，腦裏一片空白，完全不在狀態！

Valerie

原來是打機加咖啡，真太糟糕了！

Danny

這真是一個大教訓了！

意思是要教訓做錯事的人，並可以作為一些忠告，希望對方將來不要重犯。亦可用 "learn a lesson"，意指從一個不好的經驗或闖了禍而得到了教訓。

1) Kevin is well-known for his kung-fu. Trying to challenge him would probably end up being taught a lesson!

2) I should have practiced more for the speech contest. I forgot one whole line while I was giving my speech during the Contest. This has taught me a lesson!

3) I ate two ice-creams every day during my summer holiday. I will have gained five kilograms by the time I go back to school in September. What a lesson I've learned!

4) We have done so much harm to the environment. Nature will teach us a lesson.

5) I thought I was good at Chinese and didn't really care about the exam. I ended up failing the exam which has taught me a lesson!

又快又勁

Fast and furious

 學校運動會後。

Sharon

Hi, Malcolm! Many congratulations on your terrific results at our Sports Day this year. I heard you've won the 100 metres and the long jump.

Malcolm

Thanks, Sharon! I had plenty of training before the day and I did enjoy the games very much.

Sharon

So what's your coming challenge?

Malcolm

December's weather is perfect for running. I have enrolled in the half-marathon for charity. It starts at the Peak early in the morning. I'm now having regular training at a runners' club every Friday to prepare for this event.

Sharon

I am look forward to seeing you running **fast and furiously** towards the finish line on that day!

Sharon

Malcolm，聽說你在今年的運動會表現出色，贏得一百米短跑和跳遠冠軍。恭喜你！

Malcolm

多謝你，Sharon！我比賽前練習充足，比賽當天也覺得很享受啊！

Sharon

你下一個目標是什麼？

Malcolm

十二月的天氣最適宜跑步，我已經參加了半馬拉松比賽，是一項慈善長跑活動，由山頂開始。我現在參加了跑會，每逢星期五晚上練習，備戰半馬。

Sharon

真期待看見你衝過終點時**又快又勁**的樣子。

意思是充滿幹勁、快速地進行或完成一件事情或任務。這通常用來形容做事時的情況和態度，例如速度、迫切性等。早前有一系列十分叫座的荷李活電影以此諺語取名。內容描述幾個能駕駛高速跑車的人勇挫壞人的故事，相信都是利用此諺語來形容主角和車的速度及能量！

1) Approaching the end of the Swimming Gala, the swimming competition was going fast and furiously.

2) "This is a new car, please try not to go fast and furiously in it!" said Paul's mum.

3) The chefs and waiters are working fast and furiously during lunch hours to serve the customers.

4) The deadline of this project is only a few days away. You've got to work fast and furiously to meet it.

5) I just realized that I've forgotten to bring my candidate card for the open exam. I really need to run back home fast and furiously to fetch it!

November - December

Exams
Open Exams (1)

響起警號 / 亮起紅燈

A wake-up call

背景　Emily 英文科考試不合格，剛碰上班主任 Miss Cheung。

Miss Cheung

Emily, I want to know more about what has happened to you recently. I notice that you aren't doing so well in this exam. Is there anything I can do to help you?

Emily

Miss Cheung, I'm really sorry about this. It seems that I haven't done too much these days, except watching YouTube!

Miss Cheung

I see! I understand that watching YouTube can be more interesting than doing homework or revising for exams. But you have to resist the temptation and be self-disciplined. This year is particularly important to you for your secondary school allocation.

Emily

I know. What should I do now?

Miss Cheung

You have failed in your English exam. **This is a wake-up call**! You have to work harder and have better time management. Stay away from your computer unless absolutely necessary!

Miss Cheung

Emily，我想了解你最近在學業上是否出現了一些問題呢？你最近一次的考試成績退步了不少。我有什麼可以幫你呢？

Emily

真對不起，Miss Cheung！都是我不好，整天只顧上網看 YouTube，好像什麼事也沒有做過似的！

Miss Cheung

原來如此！我很明白上網看 YouTube 是很有趣的，當然要比做功課和溫習考試來得吸引，但你一定要努力抗拒誘惑和學懂自律啊！今年對你特別重要，會影響中學派位的。

Emily

我明白，但我應該怎樣做呢？

Miss Cheung

這次英文科考試不合格，情況已經**亮起了紅燈**，你要多加努力，做好時間管理，如非必要，考試期間要少碰電腦啊！

意思是發生了一些事情以作警號。通常人們依着自己的喜好行事，久而久之便會成為習慣，忽略了可能帶來的後果或傷害。"Wake-up call" 就是一個警報系統，防範於未然，就像旅行時在睡覺前都會預設一個「響鬧提示」，以防睡過頭！

1) The increased school shootings in America are a wake-up call to the Government to exercise control on the ownership of weapons.

2) Janice has failed a subject in her formative assessment since she has begun playing online computer games in summer. This is her wake-up call!

3) Cindy's overtime work and her high blood pressure since are a wake-up call for her health.

4) Peter loves running marathons, but his latest foot injuries are a wake-up call for his future practices.

5) Climate change is happening already. Isn't this a wake-up call to our lifestyle?

3.2

付出多一分力

Going the extra mile

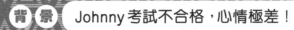

背景　Johnny 考試不合格，心情極差！

Johnny

I'm never good at things. I just know I'm not good enough. I know I'd end up nothing in future. I know...

Mandy

Please stop being so negative, Johnny! You'll be okay! It's just an exam that you've failed, not your life!

Johnny

But this exam is really important to me. I haven't thought of failing it in the first place. Looks like I have to re-take it! I feel bad about this now and things are not on my side. I don't think I can get over it.

Mandy

Don't worry! I'll come and see you now.

Johnny

Are you sure? I live in Cheung Chau and you're in Quarry Bay!

Mandy

It doesn't matter because it's worth **going the extra mile** to see you.

Johnny

我做什麼事情都不成事的！我知道我總是不夠好的！我將來一定一事無成！我肯定……

Mandy

Johnny，你別這麼負面吧！你其實一點問題都沒有，你只是一次考試不合格，而不是人生不合格！

Johnny

但是這個考試對我來說是很重要的，想不到會不合格，看來要重考了！我現在真的很難受，什麼都好像跟我過不去似的，這關真難過！

Mandy

別擔心！我現在過來看你。

Johnny

是真的麼？我住在長洲，你住在鰂魚涌，路途這麼遙遠！

Mandy

沒關係，為好朋友**多走一步**都是值得的！

意思是付出多一點努力來換取好一些的成績或報酬。諺語中的 "go" 一字可以用 "travel" 替代，而 "mile" 亦可換上 "yard" 一字。

此諺語源自《新約聖經》馬太福音五章四十一節。耶穌走遍加利利，傳天國的福音和醫治百姓的疾病，有許多人從各地來跟着他。耶穌教導人們，說：「有人想要告你，要拿你的裏衣，連外衣也由他拿去；有人強迫你走一里路，你就同他走二里。」大意是要甘心地多付出，不可推辭。

1) Our teacher cares so much about us. He goes the extra mile to teach us after school before exams.

2) Sophie is willing to go the extra mile to listen to her friends whenever they feel unhappy.

3) My mother is quite busy already, but she still goes the extra mile to help her friends with problems.

4) I appreciate people who do not just care about themselves, but are willing to go the extra mile to help improve our society.

5) Herbert is a smart kid. He always goes the extra mile when it comes to competitions.

如履薄冰

Skating on thin ice

 背景 Johnny 數學測驗的前一天，他還在看電視看過不停！

Mum

Johnny, what programme are you watching on TV? You've been watching it since you came home from school today.

Johnny

It's a movie about dinosaurs. There's a scene about a fierce dinosaur eating a man. Looks so real!

Mum

Hmm! But I remember you're having a Maths test tomorrow? Have you revised for it?

Johnny

Don't worry, Mum! I think there will be lots of questions on algebra this time. You know I'm good at algebra!

Mum

Well, you're skating on thin ice, Johnny! I think you'd better spend some time revising for your test before you take it tomorrow.

Johnny

Okay, Mum!

Mum

Johnny, 你在看什麼電視啊？你放學回家便一直看到現在，沒有停過！

Johnny

是恐龍大作戰啊！真好看！裏面有一幕是恐龍吃人的，拍得很逼真。

Mum

哦！但你明天不是有數學測驗嗎？你溫習好沒有？

Johnny

媽咪，別擔心！這一次測驗一定有很多幾何的題目。你知道我一向最醒幾何的計算法！

Mum

Johnny, 你真的冒險得**如履薄冰**！你最好都是花多一點時間溫習測驗吧！

Johnny

知道了，媽咪！

這是一個非常生動的諺語，用來表達情況險峻，有如在薄冰上溜冰，驚險萬分。請留意是溜冰，不要換上其他活動，如在薄冰上 "running" 或 "fishing"！

1) Why did you lie to your boss about your sales performance? You're skating on thin ice.

2) Grandpa still smokes a lot even after being discharged from hospital only a few days ago. He's really skating on thin ice.

3) "You look gorgeous with this dress!" "Thanks, it's my mum's, but she doesn't know!" "Oh! You're skating on thin ice, Tanya!"

4) Jenny is skating on thin ice since she lied to her teacher that she was sick.

5) If you want to go hiking alone on this rainy day, you're really skating on thin ice.

賞心悅耳 / 合心水

Music to somebody's ear

背景 Felicia 正期待着鋼琴第八級的考試成績。

Felicia

Mum, has my piano teacher called you? Why does it take so long to get the result of my Grade 8 Piano exam?

Mum

I think I've missed a call just now. Let me check! Perhaps it's from the teacher.

Felicia

Mum, I am really looking forward to the results. You know I've put so much effort towards it!

Mum

Oh! It was really the piano teacher's call that I've missed. But she's left a message. She said you got distinction! She even asked if you would want to move onto the Diploma!

Felicia

Wow! This is like **music to my ears**. Thanks, Mum!

Felicia

媽咪，鋼琴老師打了電話給你沒有？為什麼等了這麼久還沒有八級琴試的成績呢？

Mum

我剛剛漏接了一個電話，等我看看是不是她打來的！

Felicia

媽咪，我真的很心急想知成績啊，你知道我練得好辛苦啊！

Mum

唉！原來真的錯過了鋼琴老師的電話，但她留下口訊，說你琴試得了優異成績。還問你會不會繼續考演奏級呢！

Felicia

對我來說，這個消息真是**賞心悅耳**！

意思是聽到好消息，就像聽到悠揚悅耳的樂章一樣，內心無限喜悅，歡喜萬分。有時候父母聽見自己孩子玩樂時快樂的聲音，也會覺得像音樂般動聽呢！

1) When the teacher announced that I've got the highest score in the English exam, it was music to my ears.

2) Victor's encouraging words are always music to Amy's ears.

3) It's such good news that Malcolm's first choice university has offered him a place. This is really music to his ears.

4) Chloe's class teacher said that there's a good chance that she will receive a scholarship from the school. This really is music to her ears.

5) My friend has agreed to travel with me in this summer holiday. It's music to my ears.

給一些甜頭

Butter somebody up

背景 Chloe 預備了生日禮物給爸爸。

Chloe

Dad, see what I've bought you as your birthday present?

Dad

How nice! Let me see what's inside this gift box. Wow! Three beautiful pairs of socks! Thanks so much, Chloe.

Chloe

I noticed that your socks have got holes in them. I'm sure these new socks are useful to you.

Dad

How observant!

Chloe

By the way, Dad, I think my mobile phone will break down soon. I can't access my music files now. Can I have an iPhone this time? Everybody in my class has got one.

Dad

Oh, Chloe! Then I'm not the only one you have to butter up. What would your mum say?!

Chloe

Dad！看看我買了什麼給你做生日禮物？

Dad

真好，有禮物收。讓我看看盒裏是什麼？原來是三對漂亮的襪子！真合我心意，多謝你！

Chloe

我留意到你穿的襪子破了幾個洞，所以便想送襪子給你，一定用得着。

Dad

觀察力真好！

Chloe

說起來，我的手提電話快要壞了。我不能啟動音樂庫聽歌！其實我想換部 iPhone 啊！我的同學每人都有一部！

Dad

Chloe，只**給我甜頭**不夠的，還要過媽咪那一關呢！

意思是做一些事情或用一些說話來討好別人，使他答應幫忙或支持，又或者在說壞消息時不至被責罰。有說此諺語真的出自塗牛油麵包時，牛油豐厚順滑，就像向別人說美言一樣順滑流暢。

1) Chloe tries to butter up her dad before telling him she's failed her Maths test again!

2) My colleague is always buttering up the boss because she wants to have a job promotion.

3) Even if I butter up my mum, I would still need my dad's money for the new dress.

4) My girlfriend always butters up her mum by telling her she looks young.

5) Our domestic maid buttered up my mum last night by being very hardworking. She wanted to borrow money from her!

突飛猛進

By leaps and bounds

背景　Valerie 在校際朗誦比賽中獲得冠軍。

Miss Cheung

Many congratulations to you on your outstanding performance at the Speech Contest yesterday. You are the champion in your session and this is remarkable!

Valerie

Thanks for your kind words, Miss Cheung! And thank you for teaching me. I took your advice and really enjoyed the Contest. Things came so naturally when I was delivering the speech. No stage fright at all!

Miss Cheung

Good to hear that you enjoyed every moment of it. Remember you were once shy and nervous, now you have progressed **by leaps and bounds**. Well-done, Valerie!

Miss Cheung

恭喜你在昨天的朗誦比賽得到冠軍，你在組別裏是表現最出色的，做得好，非常讚賞你！

Valerie

多謝你，**Miss Cheung**！更多謝你教我如何預備這次比賽。我聽了你的建議，十分享受比賽過程。當我朗誦時所有事情都來得很自然，真的一點兒緊張都沒有。

Miss Cheung

我真開心你能享受每一刻。記得你以前是個頗害羞和緊張的女孩子，現在的你已經**突飛猛進**，脫胎換骨了。

意思是有了很大的進步。"Leaps" 同 "bounds" 都是指跳躍時的「遠」和「高」，同時用就有了加倍的效果，由莎士比亞時代一直沿用到今天了。

1) I have taken an English course at a good learning centre recently. My teacher said my writing skills have improved by leaps and bounds.

2) Due to an increased number of tourists coming to Hong Kong, total sales volume of the retail industry has grown by leaps and bounds.

3) My Maths teacher asks me to stay after school to attend a special tutorial class every week. Thanks to her help my exam scores have increased by leaps and bounds.

4) Malcolm loves running and has joined a runners' club recently. Under professional coaching, he has exceeded his personal best by leaps and bounds.

5) My mum planted some flowers a few weeks ago. She put them near our window and waters them every day. Now the flowers are growing by leaps and bounds.

給分了心／忘了形

To be carried away by something

背景　Malcolm 剛收到被英國大學取錄的消息。

Mum

Mal, how's your work? You've been studying since 8 o'clock this morning. It's now two already. You must be very hungry now. Take a break and have lunch!

Malcolm

Mum, I've tried my best to concentrate but I just can't focus on my work!

Mum

Why? I know DSE is very important to you, but don't give yourself too much pressure.

Malcolm

Don't worry, Mum! I think it's because of the good news from the university in the UK. I'm still feeling quite excited now and am **being carried away by the news.**

Mum

Malcolm，你怎麼了？你由今早八點鐘一直溫習到現在兩點鐘，就連午飯也未吃，你一定很肚餓了，來休息一下吧！

Malcolm

其實我已經用心溫習，但不知怎的總是難以集中精神。

Mum

真的嗎？我知道 DSE 對你來說很重要，但都不要給自己太大壓力啊！

Malcolm

放心吧！我想我都是因為英國大學給我的好消息，我仍覺得很興奮，**給分了心！**

亦可寫成 "get carried away"，意思是被某些人或事分了心，心臆是極度愉快和投入的，但有時候會用來作提醒，甚至諷刺之用。例如，提醒別人不要因為籌辦婚禮時得意忘形而超出預算，可以說："Don't get too carried away by the wedding and end up over-spending"。

1) When decorating for the Christmas Party, Rachel got really carried away by the glitter and sprinkled it everywhere.

2) Jack loved reading his book so much he got carried away and forgot to eat dinner.

3) Dad was being carried away when he was watching the World Cup at midnight.

4) Mum easily gets carried away by touching stories.

5) When the main actor and actress saw each other again at the airport after so long, they were completely carried away!

Christmas,

Chapter 4

December - February

New Year, CNY

守口如瓶
Lips are sealed

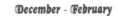

背景　Mandy 和 Jessie 是在同一間學校讀書的一對好朋友。

Mandy

Jessie, I want to tell you something. Have you got time now?

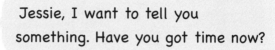

Jessie

Sure! What's up? You look so serious!

Mandy

I've just received an offer from another school.

Jessie

I see! This really took me by surprise since you've never shown any signs of wanting to leave this school! So, have you made up your mind? Will you accept this offer?

Mandy

Well, I think I will! My Mum and Dad want me to study at that school which is much nearer to my home. My parents will notify our Headmaster tomorrow. But I don't want anybody to know about this now.

Jessie

Sure. Trust me, Mandy! **My lips are sealed!** But I'm sure I'll miss you a lot!

Mandy

Jessie，我有一件事想告訴你，你現在有時間嗎？

Jessie

你神色凝重，看來好像有什麼似的。

Mandy

我剛收到另一間學校的通知，他們取錄了我做插班生。

Jessie

原來如此！這消息真來得令我驚訝，因為你從來沒有表示過想轉校！你已經確定了轉往那間學校嗎？

Mandy

我父母希望我可以轉往那一間學校，因為較接近住所。他們明天會通知我們校長，但我暫時不想其他同學知道這件事啊！

Jessie

放心，Mandy，我會守口如瓶！但我以後一定會很掛念你啊！

這個諺語十分形象化，就像一張嘴巴被封住了一樣，不會透露任何事，是守口如瓶的意思。通常是指人們想保守秘密，或未到時候告知別人。

1) "Don't worry! I won't tell anyone about your embarrassment inside the train. My lips are sealed," promised David.

2) "I'm sorry I cannot tell you what we are planning for your birthday. My lips are sealed." said one of his friends.

3) The teachers won't say anything about the upcoming tests. All their lips are sealed tight!

4) Dave's lips are sealed when asked whether he is dating Rose.

5) The Legislative Councillor's lips are sealed when the media keep asking her when she would run for election again.

得力助手／左右手

Right-hand man

背景 Ted 在學校遇上能幹的 Chloe。

Ted

Hi Chloe! I don't understand how you can manage to do so many things at the same time.

Chloe

Thanks for your kind words. But I'm not doing anything extraordinary, Ted. It's just a few small things!

Ted

Just a few small things? You're chairing the Student Union, writing our School Bulletin and organizing a sales booth at the flower market in Victoria Park this year. And you are sitting for the Piano Grade 8 exam in December, too. I just wonder how you can do it!

Chloe

Thanks, Ted. I see this as a compliment! In fact, you don't know I have a **right-hand man**.

Ted

Who?

Chloe

It's Sharon! She's the Vice-Chairman of the Student Union and an active member of the School Bulletin Committee. She's been helping me quite a lot these days.

Ted

Chloe！我真不明白你如何可以同時應付這麼多工作。

Chloe

過獎了！都沒有什麼特別，只是幾件小事情而已！

Ted

幾件小事情？你是學生會會長，又要寫校刊，今年將要組織在維園花市擺攤檔，你十二月還要考八級琴試。你是如何應付的？

Chloe

謝謝你誇獎，其實我有個**得力助手**。

Ted

誰？

Chloe

Sharon！她是學生會副會長，又是校刊委員會的活躍成員，她是我的**得力助手**！

Right-hand man 通常是指一個在工作上最能夠幫助你的人。因為一般來說，人的右手是比較強壯和靈活的，能夠完成很多工作。亦有說法是在十七、十八世紀時，有指揮軍銜的士兵都會被安排站在戰馬的右邊，以顯示其地位。在用法上並沒有分男性或女性，即是說一個女助手亦可以被稱為 right-hand man，但亦有人會刻意用 right-hand woman 來突顯是女性助手。

1) In his group of friends, Theo was the right-hand man to the Head Prefect. He helped him with everything.

2) "I know you are his right-hand man and you can influence what the manager thinks. Please tell him we prefer Osaka to Phuket for our meeting." begged the team.

3) As Miss Cheung's right-hand man, Agnes has the ability to understand what Miss Cheung wants at any given moment.

4) Our manager is always in meetings. Jennifer is not only his secretary, she's also his right-hand man.

5) The Chinese New Year party was so successful this year. Mandy is the right-hand man of the organizing department.

搶了鏡

Steal the show

背景

Katherine 將會在聖誕聯歡會上演出話劇。

Chloe

You shouldn't feel too nervous about the drama performance at our Christmas Party next month. You were great at the rehearsal.

Katherine

Thank you, but I'm still thinking about how to act more naturally on the stage! You know it is supposed to be the climax of the show!

Chloe

By the way, I've watched the rehearsal of Lucia's violin solo. She can play it so well that there's no doubt about her being the diploma holder of the instrument.

Katherine

Yes, I heard she's learning from a master and she practises for long hours every day. She's sure to steal the show that day!

Chloe

下個月聖誕聯歡會的舞台劇，你不需要太緊張啊！你的綵排表現很好。

Katherine

多謝你，但我仍想在舞台演出更加自然，因這個表演是整個聯歡會的壓軸。

Chloe

其實我還看了 Lucia 的小提琴獨奏。她實在拉得出神入化，不愧為演奏級人馬！

Katherine

我聽講她跟大師級學的，而且每天都練習。表演當日如果她能保持水準，誰也會被她**搶了鏡**！

如果要形容一位電影或舞台劇演員搶了其他人的鏡，你很容易便會聯想起照相機的鎂光燈在閃過不停，或是舞台上的燈光照射在主角身上。這個諺語用來形容蓋過了別人的風頭，而成為了一個場合或事情的焦點，其實類似的說法還有 "steal the spotlight" 或 "steal the limelight"。

1) "I know you love the attention and showing-off, but it is Ben's birthday, please try not to steal the show." said Victor.

2) Chloe has worked so hard overnight to complete her science project, yet Jane's expensive equipment and professional presentation stole the show.

3) The MCs of the opening ceremony were spectacular. They have stolen the show in every way.

4) There are always experts who can advise you how to steal the show during group interviews.

5) "I know Michelle is a good friend to you, but she'll steal the show if she becomes your bridesmaid." advised Jamie.

靈魂人物

Life and soul of the party

背景 Malcolm 和 Valerie 在籌備學校一年一度的大型環保運動。

Malcolm

Our school's annual "Save the Environment" campaign is going to take place in December. It's about time that we found someone to do the fundraising.

Valerie

Yes, I think we should. Do you have anyone in mind?

Malcolm

Well, I think Henry can do this job well. I've known him quite well. He's very sociable. He knows a lot of people.

Valerie

Well, it'd be perfect, if he is willing to help.

Malcolm

He's always the **life and soul of the party**. I'm confident that he can persuade many people to donate money to the campaign.

Valerie

No problem. Let's talk to him and see if he would like to participate.

Malcolm

學校的環保運動十二月開始，是時候找同學準備籌款活動了。

Valerie

對呀，你有人選嗎？

Malcolm

我覺得 Henry 是合適人選。我跟他頗熟落，他懂社交，又認識很多人。

Valerie

如果他肯幫手就好極了！

Malcolm

Henry 常常是工作上的**靈魂人物**，我有信心他可以說服很多人捐款支持這項活動。

Valerie

無問題，乾脆跟他談一談，希望他會一起參與！

靈魂人物就是重要人物的意思，通常指能夠在社交場合上談笑風生，能言善舞，令到在場的人都感受到愉快的氣氛。美國人乾脆用 "life of the party" 來表達同一意思。

1) At Jack's celebration, the waterslide and trampoline are the life and soul of the party.

2) Charlotte's really the life and soul of the party. Everyone loves seeing her pretty face and talking to her about things.

3) The charity benefit could not have gone on without Mr. Jonas. He donated the most money and helped out the most. He is the life and soul of the party.

4) Steve is definitely the life and soul of the party. He's trying to entertain people by engaging them in his magic show now.

5) Ivy is not only the MC of the school orientation, she's also the life and soul of the party by leading games and telling jokes.

如火如荼

In full swing

背景 同學在計劃聖誕節目。

Mandy

Hi, Malcolm! Have you got any holiday plans this Christmas? Richard and I want to go camping. Will you join?

Malcolm

I'm sorry I can't join you. My family usually goes on holiday in August, but this year we're going to Vancouver during Christmas for two weeks.

Mandy

I see. Sounds exciting! But why so different this year?

Malcolm

My cousin's getting married at Christmas. We're all attending his wedding ceremony. But my mum will fly there first to help my uncle's family. I heard there's a lot to do and the preparation is in full swing already.

Mandy

So to you, this is going to be a white Christmas!

Mandy

Malcolm! 你今年聖誕節有沒有節目呀？Richard 和我計劃露營，你有興趣參加嗎？

Malcolm

Sorry！我不能參加了。我們一家通常會在八月才外遊，不過今個聖誕節我們會去溫哥華兩個星期啊！

Mandy

為什麼今年會大大不同呢？

Malcolm

我的表哥會在聖誕節結婚，我們一家會出席他的婚禮。我媽媽會早一點出發幫舅父一家打點一下，聽說他們的準備工作已是**如火如荼**！

Mandy

你今年可以過一個白色聖誕了！

"In full swing" 本是用來形容一個人的身體在擺動的樣子，用作諺語通常是指舞會或派對已開始了，各人興高采烈。但亦經常用來形容工作已經進行得如火如荼。

1) By the time Jane and her friends got there, the party was in full swing – the music was blasting and everyone was dancing.

2) As soon as our grandparents arrived at the Christmas celebrations and we started eating, the dinner was in full swing.

3) If you want to join the hiking tour, you must sign up quickly. The enrolment is already in full swing!

4) With only six months to go, the election campaign for the Presidency is in full swing.

5) The renovation works of our school will be in full swing in summer to prepare for the new academic year.

保守秘密 / 不張揚

Between you and me

 背景　Jessie 發現了好友 Sharon 的秘密！

Jessie

Do you know Pierre and Sharon are dating each other?

Mandy

Are you kidding, Jessie? This can't be true! I think this is just rumour. Pierre has a girlfriend already!

Jessie

This is not a rumour. I actually saw them holding hands inside a shopping centre. They were shopping for Christmas presents. They looked really sweet!

Mandy

Have you told other people?

Jessie

No! Sharon is our good friend. If she doesn't tell us this means she doesn't want other people to know yet.

Mandy

Alright! So this is just between you and me.

Jessie

你知道 Pierre 和 Sharon 在拍拖嗎？

Mandy

Jessie，別說笑吧！怎可能呢？這大概是謠傳吧！Pierre 已經有女朋友了！

Jessie

這可不是謠傳啊！是我親眼看見他們在商場手拖着手選購聖誕禮物的！

Mandy

那麼你有沒有告訴其他人呢？

Jessie

沒有。Sharon 是我們的好朋友，她連我們都沒有講，她一定不想其他人知道的。

Mandy

好的，多謝你告訴我，我們就不張揚，替她**保守秘密**。

如果你或對方在說話前講 "Between you and me"，代表即將說一些秘密，希望對方聽了也不要再與其他人分享。美國人會在前面加上一個 "just" 字，即 "Just between you and me"。若是把秘密講給超過一個人聽，可以說 "between ourselves"。

1) Between you and me, after all his practising, Tom was sure to win gold for the 100m sprint today.

2) "Oh, I know how hardworking Pierre is, but between you and me, I think he just wants to beat Peter in the exam!" exclaimed Ted.

3) "As for the plans for this project, please keep the details between you and me. I don't want the other teams to know of our ideas." said Penny.

4) Just between you and me, I heard from our secretary that Tanya has just resigned.

5) Dad told Chloe, "Between you and me, I've bought this diamond ring for mum on our anniversary. See how beautiful it is!"

School &

Chapter 5

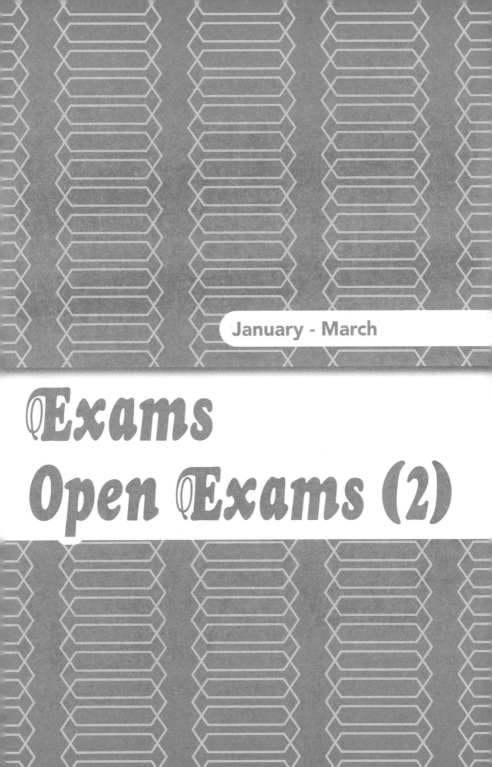

January - March

Exams
Open Exams (2)

熟能生巧

Practice makes perfect

背景　Felicia 即將應考鋼琴試第八級。

Mum

Felicia, your Piano Exam is only a few weeks from now, do you need to spend more time on preparing?

Felicia

Mum, this exam is really difficult. These three songs are hard to learn, and I can't play them well enough.

Mum

I can understand this! I know you've been trying hard, but practice makes perfect. You know I can play well, if you need my help in practising, I'm always here to fully support you.

Mum

Felicia，你的鋼琴考試快到了，這幾個星期你需要多加練習啊！

Felicia

媽咪，這個考試真難，那三首考試歌的難度很高，我總是彈得不好！

Mum

Felicia，我明白的！我知道你已經很努力，但**熟能生巧**。我的鋼琴彈得不錯，如果你想我與你一起練習，我一定會全力支持你的！

意思是常常重複做一件事會令你對這件事瞭如指掌，表現更出色。英文的 "Practice" 和 "Perfect" 都是 "P" 字開始，唸上口也容易得多！

1) Mum arrived home to the sounds of Rick playing the cello again. Rick was sure proving that practice makes perfect.

2) In the week before her exams, Jennifer wrote and rewrote all her Exam Practices, because practice makes perfect.

3) In the hope of getting a better grade for English Language at DSE, Candy has done all the Past Papers because practice makes perfect.

4) Often, you can find Annie in the ice rink practising her jumps. She knows practice makes perfect, especially for the ice-skating final.

5) In order to be able to give a good presentation at the ceremony, Ken takes fifteen minutes to speak in front of a mirror every day for two months. He knows well that practice makes perfect.

大難不死 / 險過剃頭

A close shave

背景 Christina 和朋友 Lucia 在閒談。

Christina

Hi, Lucia! I know you've just bought a new car. Is it good?

Lucia

Oh yes, it's on a promotion, so it's value for money. I'm driving my daughter to school every morning. This saves her thirty minutes at least.

Christina

I see. But I know that her school is at a steep hill. Is it easy to drive there?

Lucia

Oh yes, since you mentioned it! The other day, while I was waiting for the traffic lights to turn green on a slope, the taxi in front of me rolled back suddenly.

Christina

Oh my goodness! What did you do then?

Lucia

There was a car right behind me and there was nothing I could do. Luckily, it stopped just inches from the front of my car. It was a close shave!

Christina

Lucia，我知道你剛買了一輛新車，滿意嗎？

Lucia

因為碰巧是推廣期，所以是超值的！我每天都會送女兒上學，那樣她可以多睡半小時啊！

Christina

原來如此！但她學校在斜坡上，駕車容易嗎？

Lucia

說到斜坡，那天車子在紅綠燈前停下，前面的士突然溜後。

Christina

天啊！那你怎辦？

Lucia

我後面已緊貼另一輛車，我是沒什麼可以做的，幸好那輛的士在我的車前面幾吋停了下來。真是**險過剃頭**！

意思是情況危險，差一點便遇到意外或過不了關，但最終都是有驚無險。這個諺語十分生動，本是用來形容男士剃鬍鬚時差點兒剃到臉，頗驚險呢！這裏面的 "shave" 一字亦可以改作 "call" 一字。

1) "That was a close shave!" said Dad, after manoeuvring the car past a big lorry.

2) Sharon could not have possibly known that it was Chloe placing a surprise present in her room for her party, but it was a close shave indeed.

3) In his Science test, Johnny earned a 50%, a close shave from an F.

4) Clement has over-spent a lot in his graduation trip. He could just manage to buy his ticket back to Hong Kong. What a close shave!

5) "Don't cross the road when the red light is on. It was such a close shave when you rushed across it just now!" warned his mum.

講多無謂，行動最實際！

Actions speak louder than words

背景 Johnny 的中期考試快到了！

Mum

Johnny, have you revised for your mid-term exams? They're approaching and I heard that the papers were quite difficult last year.

Johnny

Mum, I have made a good plan on how to study already. This is my timetable for every subject, and this is another timetable on when to practice playing the piano. And this is yet another timetable on when to do exercise......

Mum

Wow, I'm impressed, Johnny! But more importantly, you need to implement your plan, because **actions speak louder than words**.

Mum

Johnny, 你的中期考試快到,你溫習好沒有?聽說上一年的考試卷很難。

Johnny

媽咪,我已一早預備了一個溫習計劃。你看,這是每一科的溫習時間表,而這一個是我的練琴時間表。我還有一個做運動的時間表呢!

Mum

Johnny,你真棒!但無論如何,記得要好好實行計劃,因為**行動最實際**!

意思是就算心裏想怎樣做、口裏說得有多動聽，始終都是行動才是最可靠的。這是一個生動的形容，因為大聲地把計劃說出來也不代表會付諸實行，所以倒不如以行動代替說話。有「少說話，多做事」的含意，坐言不如起行。

1) In apology, Jane made some cupcakes for Eve, proving actions speak louder than words.

2) "Just clean the house for your Mum on Mother's Day. Sometimes actions speak louder than words." said Dad.

3) Mike helped the team in winning the competition project, showing actions speak louder than words.

4) When the Chief Executive came to office, she promised to solve the housing problems. Hope her actions speak louder than words!

5) Dad has promised me a trip to Europe if I can attain good results in DSE. Mum and I said "Actions speak louder than words!"

一石二鳥 / 一箭雙雕

Kill two birds with one stone

 背景　Felicia 在忙著預備兩份英文科的功課。

Felicia

Mum! You know I have to write a film review for my English language class. At the same time, our English Literature teacher has also asked us to read a classic novel of the nineteenth century and write a book review on it. What should I do? There are only a few weeks left before the deadline.

Mum

This sounds very challenging as far as time is concerned. Let me think⋯ What about renting a DVD of the movie "Sense and Sensibility"?

Felicia

You mean Ang Lee's movie based on Jane Austen's book? Perfect! That would in fact make it easier for me to read the book. It not only helps me write the book review but also a film review. I can kill two birds with one stone now!

Felicia

媽咪，你知道嗎，我要寫一篇英文影評；同時間我們的英語文學老師又要我們看一本十九世紀的古典小說，然後再寫書評！只得幾星期時間，怎麼辦？

Mum

時間緊逼，真是頗具挑戰性！不如你租一套《理智與情感》的 DVD 幫幫手？

Felicia

你是指那套改篇自 Jane Austen 的書，由李安執導的電影？好極！這樣我看起書來也方便不少，還可以一次過完成兩份功課，真是**一石二鳥**！

意思是可以用一個方法，在同一時間解決兩個問題，就像用一塊石頭就能擊殺兩隻雀鳥，又或是射一支箭就可以獵到兩隻鵰。雖然事情做起來未必一定容易，但勝在省時方便，效果立見。

1) By winning a Science award, Eddy impressed his teachers while adding another achievement to his University application, successfully killing two birds with one stone.

2) Mum decided to pick up her new dress on her way to the supermarket, killing two birds with one stone.

3) Since we are going to Canada to see our Aunt, Mum thinks we can kill two birds with one stone and go down to New York to visit Grandpa as well.

4) Dad goes to the library at City Hall during lunch time every day to read. He can do a bit of exercise by walking up nine floors, killing two birds with one stone.

5) Elton loves sports. He's now working in a gym as a personal trainer, killing two birds with one stone.

患難見真情

A friend in need is a friend indeed

背景　Jessie 在預備一個重要的公開試。

Valerie

Jessie, why do you look so worried?

Jessie

I'm very worried about the open exam at the end of the month because its results are critical to my application to overseas universities. I have to obtain good scores here.

Valerie

I can understand your worry now. But have you done the past papers of this exam? Doing past papers is a very useful part of the preparation.

Jessie

I have, but I haven't approached the speaking parts at all.

Valerie

I can help you here. I can practise with you after school. Don't worry! You still have a little time for this.

Jessie

Thank you, Valerie! A friend in need is a friend indeed.

Valerie

Jessie，你好像很擔心似的！

Jessie

我很擔心下星期的公開考試，因為成績是用來考外國大學的。

Valerie

我明白。你做完所有的舊試卷沒有？聽說很有用的。

Jessie

除了說話部分，其他的我都已經做完了。

Valerie

我每日放學後都可以幫你練習的。你不要擔心，還有一個星期時間呢！

Jessie

謝謝你 Valerie！真是**患難見真情**。

朋友有很多類型，有些只限於吃喝玩樂，有些又只談利益，在你真正需要幫忙時就會消失得無影無蹤。但有些人則願意伸出援手，無條件幫你一把，這位就是你真正的朋友了！

1) "In my most panicked moment at the Ceremony, it was Amy that stepped up and helped me complete the tasks. A friend in need is a friend indeed." said the Play's Director.

2) When it started raining, Eve was the one who helped carry the most boxes into the new house. A friend in need is a friend indeed!

3) When my mother was very ill in the hospital, Marie was always comforting me and helped me get over it. A friend in need is a friend indeed!

4) Peter helped me with all my expenses in Beijing when I lost my wallet there. A friend in need is a friend indeed!

5) Kenneth was very sad when he lost his job last month. His friend Derek recommended him to his boss and he got offered the job. A friend in need is a friend indeed.

Easter

Chapter 6

Holidays

忙得不可開交

A lot on your plate

 Amy 看見丈夫 Victor 的書桌十分凌亂。

Mum

Wow! Look at your desk, Victor! Files and papers here and there! What's going on?

Dad

This is our sales report. This is our department proposal to the management on resources allocation. And this is the sales forecast I have to prepare for the meeting this week. Worse still, there's a PTA meeting at our daughter's school this Friday evening. I'm the Chairman and I must attend.

Mum

Poor husband! You have **a lot on your plate.** Let me make you ginseng tea now to refresh you!

Mum

嘩！Victor，你的書桌放滿文件夾和紙張，你在做什麼呢？

Dad

這是我們的營業報告。這是我們部門的資源分配建議書，還有這星期公司開會用的銷量預測。其實星期五晚還要到女兒學校開家教會會議，我是主席，一定要出席啊！

Mum

你真可憐啊！既然你**忙得不可開交**，我快快預備參茶給你提神好了！

意思是有很多工作要做或問題要解決，忙得不可開交，就像碟上的食物多得要掉出來，就算吃得完亦難消化！亦可寫作 "too much on your plate"。

1) During the last term of school the students have final exams as well as coursework to complete. There is so much on their plate!

2) Victor will help Amy cook dinner tonight, as she already has a lot on her plate – research and a report for tomorrow.

3) There is a lot on her plate, but Jane doesn't ask for help because she knows she can handle it all herself.

4) This summer is going to be hectic for the DSE students as they have a lot on their plate.

5) Dad has a lot on his plate as he has to finish all his work before going on holiday with us.

Mandy

Why are you crying, Felicia? Did you not have good results in your English exam?

Felicia

I got an "A". I'm in fact the best in the whole Form.

Mandy

Wow, well done! So why are you still crying?

Felicia

My mum said she would take me to Disneyland if I get over 90 marks in my English exam. And now I have achieved more than her expectations, but she won't **keep her word**!

Mandy

Oh, how come?

Felicia

She said I have to get 90 marks in all subjects before she'll take me there, but I only got 85 in my Chinese exam!

Mandy

Felicia，你為什麼在哭呢？你不是英文考試有好成績嗎？

Felicia

我拿了個「A」，亦是全級第一！

Mandy

你真棒！哪你還哭什麼呢？

Felicia

媽咪答應如果我拿 90 分或以上，就會帶我到迪士尼樂園。現在我的成績已超越她的期望，但她並沒有**遵守承諾**。

Mandy

怎會的？

Felicia

她說我要所有科目都取得 90 分以上才帶我去，但我的中文只取得 85 分呢！

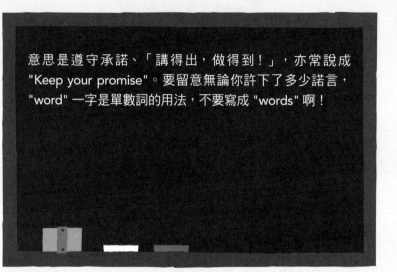

意思是遵守承諾、「講得出，做得到！」，亦常說成 "Keep your promise"。要留意無論你許下了多少諾言，"word" 一字是單數詞的用法，不要寫成 "words" 啊！

1) Mr. Poon has just announced that he would push back the deadline for our final essays. He has kept his word about being more lenient!

2) As an adult, when you promise to help someone complete a task, you have to be responsible and keep your word.

3) "We promised to help Mr. Cheung carry the footballs up the hill, we have to keep our word and do it!" said Frank.

4) The Governor has committed to solving the housing problem of the territory when she ran for election. I hope she will keep her word!

5) "Just be more patient, Jacklyn. Victor always keeps his word. If he promised to drive you to the airport, he'll be here soon!" said Amy.

6.3

我的心頭好 / 我杯茶

My cup of tea

 Katherine 同 Valerie 在計劃
農曆新年的節目。

Katherine

Hello, Valerie! Chinese New Year is coming. What do you plan to do during the school holidays?

Valerie

Well, I have to study for the mid-year exam, so I'm not doing anything particularly interesting.

Katherine

I have to prepare for the exam too, but maybe we can see a movie together. What about Japanese cartoons?

Valerie

Going to a movie sounds a good idea, but animation isn't **my cup of tea**! Shall we go for the one about space travel?

Katherine

Fine, it mustn't be boring then!

Katherine

Valerie，農曆新年快到，你在學校假期有什麼計劃呢？

Valerie

我還要預備中期考試呢，沒有什麼有趣的事做！

Katherine

我一樣要溫習考試，但看一套電影還是可以的。你喜歡日本動畫嗎？

Valerie

看電影是好主意，但動畫不是**我的心頭好**！不如看一齣有關太空漫遊的好嗎？

Katherine

沒問題，題材一定不會悶了！

香港人常說「我杯茶」，意思是自己喜歡的人或東西；喜歡的就說 "My cup of tea"，不喜歡的 "Not my cup of tea"。兩種講法都非常流行，真的易明易用！

英國人喜歡喝茶，茶葉和茶具都很講究，不少表達都會與茶扯上關係。二十世紀初，"cup of tea" 象徵品味，著名小說家 William de Morgan 在其 1908 年出版的小說 *Somehow Good* 和 Nancy Mitford 在 1932 年出版的 *Christmas Pudding* 也有用上 "cup of tea" 來形容對喜歡和不喜歡的人的感覺。

例句

1) "Ah, I can relax in this café by the sidewalk with my drink and my book. Paris is really my cup of tea!" said Jane.

2) Penny apologised for not coming to play basketball with her friends, because sports wasn't her cup of tea.

3) In winter, staying home and reading a book are always nice, but going out to have a walk is another cup of tea altogether.

4) Amy doesn't like going to that Japanese restaurant. Raw food is not her cup of tea.

5) She said she wouldn't want to see this movie because Tom Cruise is not her cup of tea.

瞭如指掌 / 滾瓜爛熟

Know someone or something inside out

 背 景　Valerie 和 Katherine 一起買衫出席聖誕派對。

Valerie

Katherine, what do you think of this dress? Do you think I should wear it at our Christmas ball?

Katherine

Well, you look lovely with this dress, and the price is reasonable. It's a good choice.

Valerie

What about you? All these dresses look so beautiful, and the ones we saw online are very nice too. But I don't think you will pick any of them.

Katherine

Why?

Valerie

Because you just don't like wearing dresses at all! You'd better buy trousers instead!

Katherine

You really **know me inside out!**

Valerie

Katherine，你覺得我穿起這條裙好看嗎？我在聖誕舞會穿它好嗎？

Katherine

好看啊！價錢又合理，的確是很好的選擇。

Valerie

你呢？這些裙子都很美，那天網上看見的也很美，不過我想你都是不會買的，對嗎？

Katherine

你又知？

Valerie

因為你最怕穿裙子嘛！你還是穿褲子罷！

Katherine

你真了解我，對我的喜好**瞭如指掌**！

意思是非常熟悉一個人、一件東西或一件事情。此諺語可以用來形容完全了解一個人的性格、喜惡、習慣等，亦可用在其他事物上如機器、程式、遊戲、步驟等。

單用 "Inside out" 可以解作一件物件或衣物的裏面和外面給反轉了。幾年前有一套流行的動畫亦以此為名，描述人的各種情緒互動對行為的影響。

1) "How did you know that these essential oils could help the kids? You do know their healing properties inside out!" said Shannon.

2) Ben used to study and work in Tokyo for a very long time. He knows the place inside out.

3) The children are worried that they will get lost in this cave, but Mrs. White assures them that she knows this cave inside out.

4) Our domestic helper has worked in our house for over ten years. She knows each one of us inside out.

5) Amy has watched all 16 episodes of this Korean TV programme many times. She knows the story inside out!

蘇州過後無艇搭

Miss the boat

Victor 帶來了好消息！

Chloe

Look at Mum, Dad. She's being carried away by her phone now.

Dad

Amy! What are you listening to? You look like you're enjoying something from your phone very much!

Mum

It's Botti's trumpet. You know I like his Boston album very much.

Dad

Of course I do. Do you know about his concert in Hong Kong?

Mum

Oh no! When is it? I didn't know! Have I **missed the boat**?

Dad

Stay calm, my dear! I just saw his advertisement at the train station. Don't worry! His concert is in five months time. To make sure we don't miss the boat, let me buy two tickets now and we can go together.

Chloe

Dad，你看媽咪拿着手機聽得多陶醉啊！

Dad

Amy，你在聽什麼？你聽得很忘形啊！

Mum

是 Botti 的小號。你一向都知道我喜歡 Botti 在波士頓演奏會的 CD！

Dad

當然。他在香港演奏你一定知道吧！

Mum

是真的嗎？什麼時候？我一點兒也不知道，我是不是錯過了？

Dad

冷靜冷靜！我剛剛在火車站看見廣告，香港演奏會是在五個月後。我立即就買兩張票，我們一起去，**免得蘇州過後無艇搭**！

是錯過了最佳時機的意思，跟中文俗語「蘇州過後無艇搭」有異曲同工之妙。錯過了的原因可以是很具體和合理的，如時間不合，亦可以純粹是不知情！喜歡「搭艇」與否，使用這諺語時也要保留 "boat" 一字，不要換上其他交通工具啊！

1) It was so unfortunate that Mrs. Chan fell sick during the last week of school. She missed the boat on the biggest farewell party from her class.

2) Flying to Europe from Hong Kong is very expensive. Check it out from time to time and don't miss the boat for cheap tickets.

3) I always miss the boat when it comes to concerts and dramas. How bad!

4) Tomorrow is the deadline for application. Act fast and don't miss the boat!

5) The car dealer is having a promotion now, so don't miss the boat if you have planned to buy one.

收入僅夠糊口

Make ends meet

背景 Felicia 剛收到學校通告，可以彈性換季。

Felicia

Mum, our school has announced that we can change to our Summer uniform beginning the second week of April on a flexible schedule. My dress is too short and my PE uniform is too small. Both my black shoes and rubber shoes are quite worn-out. Can I have new ones for all these?

Mum

Felicia, Mum knows it's uniform for the new season now, but as Dad is still looking for a job after all these months, we're just able **to make ends meet**. Why don't we buy the uniforms first and buy those shoes later!

Felicia

Okay, Mum! In fact, I also need a new schoolbag and a pencil case!

Felicia

媽咪，學校出了通告，四月第二個星期已經可以彈性換夏季校服了。我的校裙太短，運動服又太小，可以買新的給我嗎？其實我的黑鞋和運動鞋都已經很殘舊了！

Mum

Felicia，媽咪知道又快要換季了，但爸爸這些月來都找不到固定工作，要很努力掙錢**才僅夠糊口**啊！不如暫時先買校裙和運動服，遲些再買鞋罷！

Felicia

好的。其實還有書包和筆袋呢！

意思是財政緊絀，很艱難才能賺夠生活費，即收入「搵搵緊」。諺語的源起眾說紛紜，有指船杆上不同種類的繩索和連繫船杆的方法，最終都是要互相連結一起才能發揮作用；亦有說是要節衣縮食，才可以將皮帶兩邊的扣和孔穿上。亦可寫成 "make both ends meet"。

1) I know that taking on two jobs at one time is a lot, but with the increased rental, I'm just trying to make ends meet.

2) With high inflation, Peter is struggling to make ends meet for his large family.

3) In order to make ends meet, Henry has to work while studying at the same time.

4) Larry has suffered a huge loss in his stocks. He has to sell his flat and his car to make ends meet.

5) Victor's son is studying abroad this September, and his daughter will join him next year. He has to work really hard to make ends meet.

School

Chapter 7

Final Exams

挑燈夜讀 / 開夜車

Burn the midnight oil

背景 Miss Cheung 看見學生 Malcolm 精神不振的樣子。

Miss Cheung

Hi Malcolm! You look pale. Are you feeling okay?

Malcolm

I'm fine, thanks. I'm just too tired. I haven't been sleeping that much lately.

Miss Cheung

What did you stay up late for?

Malcolm

Well, you know I'm taking an exam on law. This is critical to my application for overseas universities.

Miss Cheung

What about your school exams next month?

Malcolm

I know our final examinations are coming up and time is running out. That's why I'm burning midnight oil to get things done!

Miss Cheung

Take care, Malcolm. Health is always number one!

Miss Cheung

Miss Cheung

Malcolm！你的臉色蒼白，身體不適嗎？

Malcolm

謝謝你，我沒事，只是很疲倦，近日每晚都睡得太少。

Miss Cheung

你為什麼要捱夜呢？

Malcolm

我準備報讀外國大學的法律系，很快就要考有關的公開試。

Miss Cheung

但下個月就是學校大考了！

Malcolm

我知道時間緊迫，所以我惟有**開夜車**了！

Miss Cheung

小心身體，健康為重啊！

諺語裏的 "oil"，其實是指油燈裏的油。古時沒有電燈，夜晚只好點油燈來工作。"Burn the midnight oil" 就是工作到深夜的意思，與中文「挑燈夜讀」的情景相似。

1) "You have an early start tomorrow! Try not to burn the midnight oil too much and sleep earlier." said Mum.

2) Greg loves burning the midnight oil as it is the quietest time of day and no one will disturb him as he works.

3) The midnight oil is burnt. I need to finish this paper before it's due tomorrow.

4) Tomorrow is the written part of the driving test. I have to burn the midnight oil to pass it before proceeding to the driving part.

5) In order to participate in the painting exhibition next week, Amy has to burn the midnight oil to perfect each of her exhibits.

字裏行間 / 識看眉頭眼額

Read between the lines

Our school headmaster said she is planning to send two students from our class to attend the international English competition in May.

Are you interested? Do you want to be selected? I am interested, of course! You know, this competition is extremely famous. The first three winners will be awarded a study tour in London this summer.

 學校正在挑選代表參加國際英語比賽。

Chloe

Our school headmistress said she is planning to send two students from our class to attend the international English competition in May.

Natalie

Are you interested? Do you want to be selected?

Chloe

I am interested, of course! You know, this competition is extremely famous. The first three winners will be awarded a study tour in London this summer.

Natalie

Chloe, your English is good. Everyone knows. Do you think you have a chance here?

Chloe

I don't know! I don't have the slightest clue! But my English teacher asked me to prepare a profile about myself but she didn't tell me what it was for.

Natalie

Oh, can't you read between the lines? She has you in her mind as a candidate! Congratulations!

Chloe

校長正在計劃派兩位學生出賽一項國際英語比賽。

Natalie

你有興趣嗎？想被選中嗎？

Chloe

我當然有興趣！你知道這個比賽有多出名嗎？而且頭三名勝出者可以在這個暑假免費參加倫敦遊學團。

Natalie

Chloe，我們都知你的英語一向了得，你覺得自己有機會被選中嗎？

Chloe

我怎知道呢？一點風聲也沒有！但英文老師要我準備一份個人資料，但沒有告訴我其他的。

Natalie

你還看不懂**字裏行間**的意思嗎？她也認定你是候選人了。恭喜你！

有說以前傳遞秘密訊息時會用上隱形墨水，在行與行之間寫上字，看訊息的人要用特別方法才能看出是什麼。現在用來比喻不要單看表面，要細心意會別人的文章、說話或行為背後的真正意思，即中文「看出字裏行間的意思」一樣，或所謂「識看眉頭眼額」，就是看懂別人真正心意的意思。

1) Try to read between the lines of what he's saying! He wants you to help him make the decision!

2) Kelly acts very nicely to the girls who lie, but if you read between the lines, you can tell she resents them.

3) Walter believes Rachel actually wants to go to Italy for their honeymoon, so he makes the plans, hoping he isn't reading between the lines wrongly.

4) If Bella can read between the lines, she should know that Michelle doesn't want to be her friend.

5) Maggie can read between the lines that Jonathan was asked to leave the company.

務求十拿九穩，萬無一失

Take no chances

背景 大考將近，Felicia星期日仍在苦幹！

Mum

Felicia, it's Sunday today, take a break and have a walk in the park!

Felicia

This final exam is very important to my subject application next year. I have to work harder!

Mum

You need not worry too much, 'cause you're good at most subjects.

Felicia

Well, I want to study English Literature and seats are limited. The school only picks the best. So I'm taking no chances.

Mum

Felicia，今天是星期日，不如休息一下，逛逛公園吧！

Felicia

這次大考對我明年選修科目很重要，我要加倍努力。

Mum

不用太擔心，你每科的成績都不錯。

Felicia

我想選修英國文學，學位有限，學校只會選擇成績最好的學生。所以我要加倍用功，**不作冒險，務求萬無一失**！

"Take no chances" 是不冒險、百分百肯定不會出亂子的意思。要注意 "chances" 一字是複數（plurals）的用法；至於 "take a chance" 則是剛剛相反，意思是要碰碰運氣、試試有沒有機會。

1) Malcolm made sure all his bases were covered. He took no chances when reporting to his superior.

2) Rachel decided not to take any chances with the bus this time. She would take the train.

3) I am working with the Chairman tomorrow. I am taking no chances this time!

4) I take no chances when it comes to competitions.

5) Amy has a body check-up regularly. She takes no chances with her health.

7.4

不記錄在案 / 不對外公開

Off the record

背景 Natalie 和 Mandy 好像在講秘密似的！

Natalie

I heard Johnny has failed in two main subjects in this exam.

Mandy

It's true. He's very worried about not being able to be promoted!

Natalie

I met Miss So outside the Teachers' Room yesterday. She said two students in our class will not be promoted!

Mandy

And off the record, I think Johnny is one of them!

Natalie

聽說 Johnny 今次考試有兩科主科不合格！

Mandy

是真的，他也很擔心不能升班！

Natalie

其實我昨天在教員室門口剛巧遇上 Miss So，她說我們班裏會有兩位同學留級。

Mandy

現在說的**不要記錄在案**，我看其中一個應該是 Johnny 呢！

說話前事先聲明是 "Off the record"，就是表明是不屬於官方或正式講話，希望對方不要向外界（尤其是傳媒）公開或引述，帶有保密的意思。

1) Joe keeps saying that he resigned for a better job, but off the record, he quit because he didn't get along with his colleagues.

2) "Everyone passed, but off the record, I know that there are a few people who have cheated in the test." said Jamie.

3) During the Exit interview, Peter made sure what he said about his boss would be off the record.

4) Off the record, I think Keith and Claudia are having problems with their relationship.

5) Officially, I don't know anything, but off the record, I know Michelle will win the Beauty Pageant!

變成窮光蛋 / 要破產了

Break the bank

  Mandy 的偶像來港演奏。

Ted

Hi Mandy, I've got some good news for you!

Mandy

What is it?

Ted

Your favourite Spanish classical guitarist is coming to town in two months time.

Mandy

That's really good news. But I guess the tickets must be very expensive.

Ted

It won't break the bank. I think the lowest priced ones are still available. Come on, you just can't afford to miss it.

Mandy

Thanks Ted, let's buy one after school. Will you also buy one and go with me?

Ted

Mandy，我有好消息告訴你！

Mandy

什麼好消息呢？

Ted

你最喜歡的古典結他手兩個月後
來香港表演。

Mandy

這的確是天大喜訊，但我想像門
票一定很貴！

Ted

應該不會**令你破產**的，你亦可以
考慮買最平的位置，大概仍未售完。
快買票，你一定不會想錯過的。

Mandy

多謝你，Ted！放學立刻買一張，
你會多買一張陪我嗎？

意思是花光了金錢。諺語本身用來形容有人在賭場上贏了大錢，銀碼竟然超過莊家的賭本，使賭場破產。"Bank" 一般是指銀行，但這裏是一個賭場的術語，是指莊家的賭本。現在 "Break the bank" 已變成日常用語，指破產或變成窮光蛋的意思。

例句

1) "Buying a dress at $2000 for the graduation dinner would break the bank!" exclaimed Sara.

2) Valerie thought buying a new computer would break the bank, but she has actually saved enough money to buy a new phone as well.

3) After that expensive lobster dinner, Eve and her friends couldn't afford to eat out anymore. They've broken the bank, at least for a few weeks.

4) After our holiday trip to Switzerland, we've broken the bank!

5) We would break the bank if we buy this big house in this district of the city.

風雨同路 / 不離不棄

Through thick and thin

背景　Jessie 突然感染了嚴重的疾病。

Jessie

Mandy, I really have to thank you for all your help through these difficult days of mine. Without your help and encouragement, I would not have survived the exam.

Mandy

Don't mention it. You suddenly got this serious infection and had to be bed-ridden for so long. I'm your friend; can I just stand aside and watch?

Jessie

You're really my best friend and always stick with me through thick and thin! Thank you, Mandy!

Jessie

Mandy，我真的要謝謝你，在這些艱難的日子幫助我、鼓勵我，不然我一定熬不過了。

Mandy

你突然感染了嚴重的疾病而需要長時間臥床，這段時間，我怎可以坐視不理呢？

Jessie

你真是我最好的朋友，在我有需要時**不離不棄**。謝謝你！

意思是能夠與你共渡時艱，不會因為你遇到挫折或逆境時便遠離你，跟中文的「甘苦與共」大致相同。

很久以前，英國還沒有開墾道路，要穿越四周叢林就不得不披荊斬棘。這裏的 "thick" 同 "thin"，就是指「茂密」與「疏落」的叢林。使用時記得要注意次序，是 "thick" 先、"thin" 後，是 "Through thick and thin"，不是 "Through thin and thick"!

1) Marie is my best friend, through thick and thin.

2) Husband and wife stick together through thick and thin.

3) Dad is a big fan of Williams. He is loyal to her through thick and thin, though she has lost with disgrace in her recent tennis tournament.

4) No matter how hard, my friends still support me through thick and thin.

5) The Church members have to support each other through thick and thin, regardless.

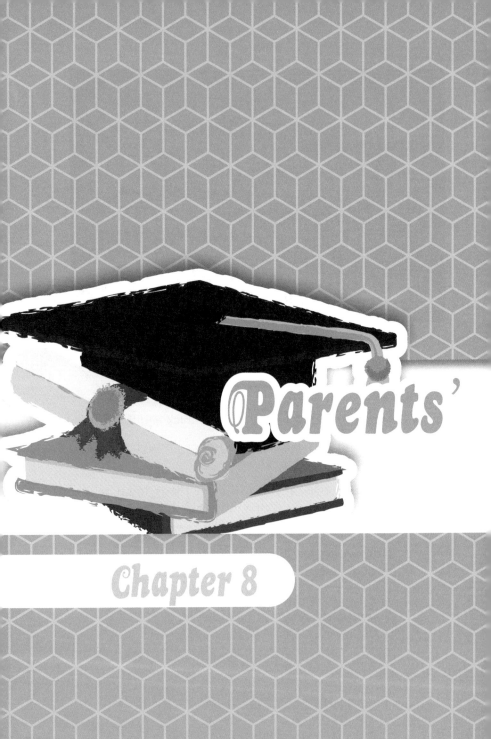

Parents'

Chapter 8

June - July

Day/
Graduation Day

帶頭做起 / 當先頭部隊

Get the ball rolling

  學校BBQ！

Mandy

This barbecue is great fun. All of us are having a really good time here. The food and games are excellent!

Natalie

I can't agree with you more. We really have to thank Miss Cheung for organizing everything for us.

Mandy

But look at her now! I think she's busy asking everyone to clean up. There's lots of rubbish and leftover food everywhere.

Natalie

As the others are still playing, I think it's a good idea that we start to help clean up. Would you help, Mandy?

Mandy

Yes, of course! If we get the ball rolling, I think they will all join in.

Mandy

這次燒烤真的好玩，食物和遊戲都一流，大家都玩個夠本！

Natalie

絕對同意！我們真的感謝張老師替我們安排得這麼周到。

Mandy

但你看，他正忙着找同學幫忙收拾垃圾和剩餘食物。

Natalie

其他同學仍在玩樂呢；不如我們**帶頭做起**，其他人看見便會加入幫忙了。Mandy，你會幫忙嗎？

Mandy

我當然會啦！我們一於做**先頭部隊**，他們也會跟着幹吧！

本來是指進行球類運動時不要把球停留在同一位置太久，應該要不停地在球場上走動傳球才是！

套用在諺語，意思是帶頭進行一件工作，不要讓它停止；亦可用在社交場合上，首先打開話匣子，與他人交談、寒暄，以展開其他活動。

1) It is rather hard to start writing an essay, but once you get the ball rolling, you'll be done in no time.

2) I wake up really early. It's better to get the ball rolling in the morning so you can finish work earlier!

3) By trying to get the ball rolling, Dad was the first one to share his story about his childhood at the dinner gathering.

4) In view of the tight deadline, Charis tries to get the ball rolling by volunteering to outline the timetable for the project.

5) Edward starts the ball rolling and comes up to the front of the class to present his findings.

不可以貌取人

Can't judge a book by its cover

 背景 在學校頒獎禮上。

Mum

Johnny, who's this boy? He's number one in your whole form and also getting most of the academic awards?

Johnny

That's Teddy, he's in my class! He's not only smart in all subjects, he's also a keen athlete and musician.

Mum

Well, he doesn't look particularly special on the outside. He's actually quite small. So don't judge a book by its cover. He's achieved great heights!

Mum

Johnny，這個男生是誰？他是你同年級第一名，囊括了多個學術獎項。

Johnny

那個是我班的 Teddy，他不單只學習了得，就連運動和音樂都很出色呢！

Mum

看他其貌不揚，個子矮小，原來文武雙全，真不可以貌取人！

此諺語形象化地描述了我們選擇書本時，往往只看封面設計是否吸引而忽略了書的內容是否合適。用來形容人也一樣，我們很容易被外表吸引或蒙騙，所以要學懂鑒貌辨色，不要以貌取人，這樣其實一點都不易啊！

1) She looks very bitter and sullen on the outside, but she is actually very nice when you get to know her. So don't judge a book by its cover!

2) Don't judge a book by its cover, the hotel is very cosy inside though it looks a bit old.

3) This learning centre is very small, but don't judge a book by its cover, its courses are well-planned and the teachers are very professional.

4) Our car is quite old, but don't judge a book by its cover, its engine is still running superbly well.

5) When it comes to choosing friends, don't judge a book by its cover. People with a sweet face may not always be good natured.

保持聯絡

Keep in touch

 畢業聚餐前夕。

Malcolm

Time flies, Chloe! Six years of school life have passed. I can still remember my first day here.

Chloe

True! Honestly, it was hard going through tests, exams and this DSE, but as the graduation dinner is approaching, my feelings are mixed.

Malcolm

We're entering another stage in life, and we'll still be friends. So, let's keep in touch!

Malcolm

時光飛逝，六年中學瞬間便成過去。我還記得第一天來到這裏的情景。

Chloe

完全同意！坦白說，測驗、考試，再加上文憑試，我覺得求學都很辛苦，但畢業聚餐在即，我仍是百感交雜的。

Malcolm

畢業後，又踏進另一個階段了，我們要**保持聯絡**，繼續做朋友啊！

"Keep in touch" 就是與人保持聯絡、繼續往來的意思。人有悲歡離合，但現在資訊科技發達，要與別人溝通、保持聯絡一點都不困難，所以離別時說一聲 "keep in touch" 都是輕鬆自然的事！"Keep in touch" 亦可說成 "be in touch"、"get in touch"、"stay in touch" 和 "remain in touch"。

1) These days you can find anyone on the internet. You can even keep in touch with your kindergarten teachers!

2) It doesn't matter that Laura was going off to America to start university. She can keep in touch with her friends from home via Facebook.

3) I'm sorry that we can't work together on this project, but please keep in touch. Other opportunities may come up in the future.

4) Edward doesn't enjoy company. He never keeps in touch with people.

5) My parents have separated, but they still keep in touch with each other.

膽戰心驚

Get cold feet

背 景 畢業禮翌日。

Valerie

Natalie, congratulations to you! You did great on stage as our MC yesterday.

Natalie

Thanks! You know it was my first time being the MC of our Graduation Ceremony. Of course, I was excited. But I got cold feet when Miss Cheung suddenly told me the other MC was sick and I had to be up on the stage on my own.

Valerie

Oh, that can't be real! Not even the slightest sign could be seen! You do have flair!

Valerie

Natalie，恭喜你！你昨天做司儀很出色啊！

Natalie

多謝你！我是第一次做畢業典禮的司儀，心情當然很興奮。但當 **Miss Cheung** 突然告訴我另一位司儀病倒了，我要獨擔大旗，我真覺得**膽戰心驚**！

Valerie

噢！是真的嗎？真的一點也看不出，你果然不怯場，很有做司儀的天份呢！

"Get cold feet" 意思是感覺惶恐、焦慮，甚至想放棄原本已計劃好的事情。有說人感覺緊張和驚慌時雙腳會瞬間變冷，因為血液都集中在心和腦。"Get cold feet" 亦可以寫成 "Have cold feet" 或 "On cold feet"。

1) Everybody's had cold feet when our teacher said half of the class have failed in the Maths exam.

2) On the day of the wedding, Freda had cold feet and didn't want to leave mum and dad.

3) Kelly got cold feet while waiting for the selection interview, and left.

4) Penelope got cold feet when it was her turn to do the presentation, and left it to others.

5) I was waiting on the roller-coaster, but I got cold feet suddenly, and jumped off.

長話短說

Cut a long story short

AaBbCcDdEeFfGg
HhIiJjKkLlMmNnOo
PpQqRrSs

背景　Mum 向 Emily 索取數學測驗卷。

Mum

Emily, your Maths test was last week, have you got the paper back?

Emily

Well, Mum, Miss Lau was sick last Thursday and Friday and the supply teacher wasn't as nice as her. His name's Mr Tam. He's a very boring person. He just read from our textbook and we had to copy the formulae from the board. No one enjoyed his lessons because we......

Mum

Emily! To cut a long story short, have you received the test paper? Did you pass?

Emily

Umm, Mum!

Mum

Emily，你上星期數學測驗，派了卷沒有？

Emily

媽咪，上星期四和星期五 Miss Lau 病了，代課老師沒有她那麼好人，他叫 Mr Tam。Mr Tam 教書好悶，只管把書一行一行的讀出來，又不解釋算式，要我們光抄黑板……我們真的不喜歡上他的課，他又……

Mum

Emily！**長話短說**，你究竟收到測驗卷沒有？你合格嗎？

Emily

唔，媽咪！

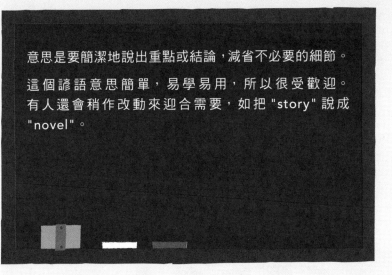

意思是要簡潔地說出重點或結論，減省不必要的細節。

這個諺語意思簡單，易學易用，所以很受歡迎。有人還會稍作改動來迎合需要，如把 "story" 說成 "novel"。

例句

1) Mum and Dad are very concerned about my education. So making a long story short, I'm studying abroad in the coming academic year.

2) We've had a good look at the houses around here. To cut a long story short, we're moving in next month.

3) I don't think we're getting along too well. So keeping a long story short, shall we part?

4) I've been busy with my work, my dear! Our Director just flew from our headquarters in New York. To cut a long story short, I can't celebrate your birthday with you tonight.

5) Jamie Oliver first started his career as a pastry chef and, to cut a long story short, he is now the owner of numerous restaurants around the world, including in Hong Kong.

Summer

Chapter 9

Holidays

大懶蟲

A couch potato

Mum

Johnny, it's ten o'clock already! Why are you still lying on your bed? It's just a few more days before your new school year begins. Have you put away your old textbooks and replaced them with new ones on the bookshelves? Also, remember to tidy your room to have a good start for the year!

Johnny

Well, as you said, there are still a few more days Mum, why bother to do it now! And more importantly, I don't think my room is messy at all!

Mum

Come on, Johnny! Your room is messy! Just look at the toys and books on the floor! And the clothes that you wore last week are still on your bed! The thing is, I've asked you to tidy your room since the beginning of the month. Look what day it is today! And see what you are doing now? Just lying in bed playing computer games! You're such **a couch potato**!

Johnny

I'm sorry, Mum! Just let me finish this game first and I'll tidy my room later. I promise!

Mum

Johnny，已經十點鐘了，你為什麼還躺在床上啊？過幾天是新學年，你整理好書架，拿走舊書再放上新書沒有，你的房間還很亂呢？

Johnny

媽媽，不用急！你說還有幾天嘛，為什麼一定要今天做呀！反正我覺得我的房間一點都不亂。

Mum

Johnny，你的房間還不算亂？一地都是你的玩具和功課簿，你上個禮拜穿的衣服還在床上！
我月初已經叫你收拾房間，而你就把我的話當作耳邊風！你仍然動也不動，懶在床上打機，真是**大懶蟲**！

Johnny

Mum，我知道了，答應你我玩完這場遊戲會收拾房間了！

任何人都有躲懶的時候，但是 "A couch potato"「大懶蟲」是用來形容非常懶惰的表現或不願動的懶人，特別用來形容只躺在沙發上看電視、玩手機、玩電腦遊戲等，一點運動、讀書、收納也不做的人！正因如此，我們用的時候請勿把 "couch" 一字改做其他東西如 bed、sofa bed 或 armchair 之類，也不要把 "potato" 一字改作其他食物！

1) My plans for the new year are always about working harder so I can get rid of being called "a couch potato"!

2) Being a personal trainer working in a gym, I have successfully turned many couch potatoes into active and healthy people.

3) Under this perfect weather, nobody wants to be a couch potato at home.

4) It has been a long hard week, and Megan has no plans for Friday night except being a couch potato and eating ice cream.

5) Don't be a couch potato during long holidays. Learn a sport and enjoy your time!

9.2

完成「手尾」

Tie up loose ends

背景 放暑假，找節目！

Manson

Chloe, Scarlett and I are going to see a film about a teddy bear tomorrow morning. Tickets are cheaper in the morning. Will you come with us?

Chloe

I can't go with you tomorrow because I have to go back to school in the morning.

Manson

Why? It's the summer holiday now. Why do you still need to go to school?

Chloe

Well, it's the House committee meeting! We will run a "Textbook Re-sale" activity end of July and we have tomorrow to tie up some loose ends.

Manson

Oh I see! Why don't we wait for you and watch this movie together the day after!

Manson

Chloe，Scarlett 和我明天早上想去看一套關於玩具熊的電影。早場的戲票會比較便宜，你有興趣一起去嗎？

Chloe

我不能去了，因為我明天早上要回學校。

Manson

現在是暑假，為什麼你還要回校？

Chloe

明天要開學社的會議。我們會在七月尾舉辦一個「舊書買賣日」，所以明天要回校**完成「手尾」**。

Manson

原來如此！那麼我們等你完成後，後天再去看吧！

這個諺語的意思是已完成大部分工作，只是需要完成一些細節和「手尾」便大功告成。此諺語用途廣泛，除了常常在公事層面，也可以用在大小事務如家課、旅行準備、裝修，甚至家務等。

這個諺語的出處，原指在船隻出海前，船員有大量工作需要準備，其中一項是要把船上的繩索繫緊，不容許有散亂鬆縛的情況，以免發生危險。

1) For the contract, Victor just has to tie up some loose ends before he can close the deal.

2) Clive told his Mum that he was tying up loose ends for his essay and wouldn't need to stay up late at night.

3) The agent told Peggy that after the workmen have tied up all the loose ends, the apartment would be ready to be rented out next week.

4) Malcolm's tying up loose ends now before leaving for his studies in London.

5) Our family goes on holiday this Saturday. We'll tie up loose ends and pack tomorrow.

傾盆大雨

Raining cats and dogs

背景　終於做完暑假功課了！

Felicia

Mum, I've just finished doing the most time-consuming project of my summer holiday homework. What a relief!

Mum

Good to hear! So have you planned anything interesting for the rest of the holiday?

Felicia

I've actually planned for camping next week, but it's been **raining cats and dogs** these days, so I'm a bit worried.

Mum

That's true! The weather will be better next week. Let's hope for the best.

Felicia

媽咪，我終於做完這份最花時間的暑期專題研習，真的鬆了一口氣！

Mum

真是好消息！你在餘下的假期有什麼計劃呢？

Felicia

我其實已經約定了同學下星期露營，但這幾天都下着**傾盆大雨**，我有點擔心呢！

Mum

那倒是真的，但下星期的天氣應該會好轉的，不用太擔心啊！

這個諺語早在 1651 年的詩已經出現，往後亦有不少作家在其作品中提及貓狗在下雨時的種種情形，但其出處則沒有定案；或許與雷神奧丁有關，因為奧丁常被繪畫成狗或狼來象徵「風」，而故事裏的巫婆是一隻騎着掃把的貓，象徵「雨」。

使用時要留意 "cats" 與 "dogs" 的先後位置，是 "raining cats and dogs"，不是 "raining dogs and cats"。這剛好與我們廣東話說的「貓貓狗狗」次序相同呢！

1) It started raining cats and dogs outside, stranding us in the restaurant.

2) Remember to bring an umbrella when you go outside in summer, as it might suddenly start raining cats and dogs.

3) "I couldn't do any work on my garden! It rained cats and dogs all weekend." moaned Dad.

4) Typhoon signal number 8 is hoisted and it's raining cats and dogs. Therefore the picnic is cancelled.

5) The renovation has to be postponed since it's been raining cats and dogs for a week.

大日子
Red-letter day

背 景 兒子快將遠赴海外升學。

Mum

Malcolm, please help me tidy up and decorate this house! We're having two gatherings this weekend to celebrate your future studies in the UK.

Malcolm

Okay, Mum! Time flies. I have to leave Hong Kong next month.

Mum

Your first day at university is your **red-letter day**. Work hard and live well, and don't forget we're all giving blessings to you!

Mum

Malcolm，快來幫忙收拾和佈置家居，今個周末有兩個聚會，都是慶祝你將到英國升學的。

Malcolm

知道！時間過得真快，下個月就要離港了！

Mum

你入大學的第一天真是個**大日子**，你要努力讀書，好好照顧自己，切勿忘記我們在這裏給你的無限祝福啊！

"Red-letter day" 指重要日子的意思。古時候教會會在日曆上以紅色標示重要的宗教日子，這種做法往後在歐洲國家亦被廣泛使用。在英國，宗教節日以外的法定假期也印上紅色，使日期在日曆上更為明顯。此外，學術界亦有稱之為 "scarlet day"。

1) It was a red-letter day to my family when we were informed of our citizenship in this country.

2) Marie and Edwin's red-letter day is at the end of this month. I'll definitely attend their wedding feast in the evening.

3) The day that my DSE results were announced was my red-letter day which I'll never forget.

4) It was really Alvin's red-letter day when his first auto body shop opened in Vancouver.

5) Today is a red-letter day for Jennifer because she's going to see her K-pop idol at the airport.

9.5

使人毛骨悚然

Make one's hair stand on end

 同學之間打賭，有人輸了！

Henry

I'm really worried, Mandy!

Mandy

What are you worrying about?

Henry

I've made a bet with Roy that if he wins the game, I'll go to Macau and try a Bungee Jump on the tower.

Mandy

Oh, Henry! You're afraid of heights, why did you make such a bet?

Henry

Why? Because I thought Roy wouldn't win! But I was obviously wrong. To everyone's surprise, he did win! Now, simply the thought of jumping down from the top of the tower has already **made my hair stand on end**!

Henry

Mandy，我正在苦惱啊！

Mandy

你在苦惱什麼呢？

Henry

我和 Roy 打賭，如果他贏了比賽，我就要去澳門塔「笨豬跳」。

Mandy

天啊！你明明畏高的，為什麼要這樣打賭？

Henry

因為我以為我贏定了！明顯地，我錯了！出乎意料地，Roy 竟然贏了！現在我只要一想到要從高塔跳下來就已經**毛骨悚然**！

這是一個很生動的形容，描述人受到驚嚇時，身體上的本能反應包括瞳孔放大、心跳加速、呼吸困難……害怕得連頭髮也豎起來！這個諺語早在十七世紀初莎士比亞的明著《哈姆雷特》已經出現了，廣東話的「驚到毛管戙」就是神形俱似的說法了！

1) As she walked into the corridor, she felt something brush against her arm, making her hair stand on end.

2) The cat shrieked as it saw a stranger. Its hair stood on end, making it look like a porcupine.

3) Inside that old mansion we heard the wind howling through the corridors. Immediately all of our hair stood on end.

4) The horror movie made Rex's hair stand on end, he swore not to watch any thrillers again!

5) Matt dived and watched the sharks under water, which made his hair stand on end.

一成不變，沒有改變的餘地

Written in stone

背景 Felicia 的中文科不合格，要留班了。

Felicia

I can't study with you in the same class next year, Valerie. I'm not promoted because I've failed in Chinese Studies.

Valerie

It's sad to hear this. It's only one subject that you've failed. In fact, they should have given you a marginal pass, or you should have appealed to our school Principal to see if he could grant you special permission to be promoted. But it's all too late now!

Felicia

Well, I did! But our school is really strict about the promotion of students. The criteria are **written in stone.**

Valerie

Work hard, Felicia! You'll be fine. I'm good at languages. I can help you whenever necessary.

Felicia

Valerie，我下一年不可與你同班了，因為我的中文科不合格，要留班了！

Valerie

這真是個壞消息！其實你只有一科不合格，又只是差一點分數，你應該懇求校長再考慮給你升班⋯⋯但現在一切都太遲了！

Felicia

其實我有請求校長，但學校的升班條件很嚴格，一切已成定局，**沒有改變的餘地**。

Valerie

那麼加油吧，Felicia！語文是我的強項，你要幫忙的話，我隨傳隨到！

意思是一切已成定局，沒有改變的空間。

在沒有發明其他記載工具如木刻、竹簡和紙張時，古人把符號和圖畫等刻在石頭上成為石刻，不容易修改或清除。《聖經》裏「十誡」是人人皆知的石刻。《聖經》記載，是神把吩咐以色列人須遵守的十條誡律寫在兩塊石版上，命令摩西從西乃山搬到山下。

"Written in stone" 亦可寫成 "Carved in stone"、"Burnt in stone" 或 "Set in stone"。

1) The two companies are still working out the details of their deal now, and nothing is written in stone yet.

2) The rules and regulations of this hall are written in stone. No exceptions will be granted to students under any circumstances.

3) Mary very much wants to have a better deal with this famous designer shop on her wedding dress but is told that all prices are written in stone and are not negotiable.

4) Voters have to abide by the laws of the election which are written in stone.

5) We want to buy an overseas property in Vancouver and have been visiting show flats these months. But nothing is written in stone yet.

Exercises

Practice Makes Perfect

LEVEL 1

Match the following idioms with the 10 correct meanings.

The Idiom

1) On cloud nine ( )

2) In full swing ( )

3) Make ends meet ( )

4) Get the ball rolling ( )

5) Make one's hair stand on end ( )

6) A lot on your plate ( )

7) Teach somebody a lesson ( )

8) Steal the show ( )

9) Practice makes perfect ( )

10) Between you and me ( )

Means...

a) Putting the ends of two ropes together.

b) Being the centre of attraction.

c) Feeling horrified.

d) Having too many things to do.

e) Feeling very nervous.

f) You are asking the other party to keep a secret.

g) Taking away something that you like.

h) Inviting someone to play football.

i) Having just enough money to buy food and pay the bills.

j) Having had a poor haircut.

k) Being eager to teach another person a new thing.

l) Swinging happily in the playground.

m) Feeling extremely happy.

n) Things are progressing in full speed.

o) Someone has to start working so that others will follow.

p) Punishing somebody for having done something wrong.

q) Eating too much.

r) Flying up high in the sky.

s) Repeating doing something so as to become very good at it.

Answers:
1) m 2) n 3) i 4) o 5) c
6) d 7) p 8) b 9) s 10) f

Exercises

Rise to the Challenge

LEVEL 2

Match each question or sentence on the left with an appropriate response on the right.

1) Is Victor the top student in your class? ( )

2) Do you think your friend will like the present you bought? ( )

3) In the end, did you manage to finish the project on time? ( )

4) I heard you're leaving. Hope we'll see each other soon. ( )

5) Dad, will you really take me to Switzerland on holiday this summer? ( )

6) Do you think Kim can understand your message clearly? ( )

a) Sure, 'cause I know this person inside out.

b) Yes, let's keep in touch.

c) You know I always keep my word.

d) I think he's clever enough to read between the lines.

e) Absolutely! He always passes with flying colours.

f) Yes, but I had to burn the midnight oil.

243

Exercises

Put on a brave face

LEVEL 3

Please choose the suitable idioms from the book to fill in the blanks below. You may need to put the words in the correct form and/or make appropriate alterations if necessary.

1) Sophia doesn't do any exercise but loves watching TV and playing computer games. Her mum always says she's a _____.

2) Legislators always make lots of promises in their election campaigns, but they should know that _____. People are watching over what they actually do.

3) Emily has been eating too much since Christmas. Her huge gain in weight is a _____ that she has to start looking at her diet.

4) Edwin is very fond of Marie. Whatever Marie says is _____.

5) This restaurant is small and doesn't look impressive from the outside. But_____, its food is the best in town.

6) I'm not watching this movie with you. Thriller is not _____.

7) Kenneth and Miranda first met at my wedding four years ago. To _____, they got married and have two children now.

8) John was very late for work this morning. No sooner than he sneaked into the office when his supervisor called for an urgent meeting. It was such a _____.

Answers:
1) couch potato
2) actions speak louder than words
3) wake-up call
4) music to his ears
5) don't judge a book by its cover
6) my cup of tea
7) cut a long story short
8) close shave

245

Notes

校園諺語全年通
English Idioms - All Year Pass!

編著
Amy Cheung

編輯
Cat Lau

美術設計
YU Cheung

錄音
Amy Cheung, Maxine Poon, Richard Wong

出版者
萬里機構出版有限公司
香港鰂魚涌英皇道1065號東達中心1305室
電話：2564 7511
傳真：2565 5539
電郵：info@wanlibk.com
網址：http://www.wanlibk.com
　　　http://www.facebook.com/wanlibk

發行者
香港聯合書刊物流有限公司
香港新界大埔汀麗路36號
中華商務印刷大廈3字樓
電話：2150 2100
傳真：2407 3062
電郵：info@suplogistics.com.hk

承印者
萬里印刷有限公司

出版日期
二零一八年十一月第一次印刷